To Monica
Best Wishes
David McElhaney

Fifteen Kids and an Old Blind Horse

David McElhaney

PublishAmerica
Baltimore

First printing

ISBN: 1-4137-9447-5
PUBLISHED BY PUBLISHAMERICA, LLLP
www.publishamerica.com
Baltimore

Printed in the United States of America

In Memory of Our Parents

Thanks to Brian McElhaney, a fifth grader, for creating the sketches that depict the theme of each chapter.

Contents

Foreword

Most people in modern times would have difficulty understanding the way millions of people lived in rural America during the nineteenth century, how they settled on a few acres of land, almost entirely earning their living from the soil. Homesteaders often settled in valleys along a creek, off the beaten path. Many homes were constructed from logs with a mud/mortar solution to fill the open spaces. Framed houses were covered with clapboards or roughly sawn lumber, and when finished, were not much more than wooden shells.

Domestic work was performed by hand labor, and horsepower was defined by the size and quality of the working animals one owned. Most agricultural plots were small, and these early settlers eked out a meager living by raising fruits and vegetables, along with feed for the domestic animals.

Our family would be atypical to the degree that we were somewhat isolated from society, living far into the hills with the nearest neighbor nearly one half mile away. In comparison to typical rural families, one could say we represented the disadvantaged who had not succeeded in keeping up with any degree of progress in the cultural, economical, or social world.

The stories of our family occurred mostly during the decades of the twenties, thirties, and forties of the twentieth century. The first period was represented by the roaring twenties, when most people in America celebrated the good times. These good times ended abruptly with the stock market crash in 1929, due to mismanagement in both the government and the industrial world. This catastrophe was followed by the Great Depression of the thirties, when unemployment reached nearly 40 percent in many parts of the country, which had a profound impact on the economic well-being of most rural families as well as the urban population. Fathers found it quite difficult to feed their families as work was scarce at most times. Proud family men who had worked all their lives in the service and industry sector of the economy and had now lost their jobs were forced to rely on public assistance for the daily necessities of life.

Many depressed families were forced to sell their homes and farms, receiving just a few cents on the dollar relative to the value of their property before the Depression. If one was fortunate enough to have money in the bank, much or all of it was lost, as most of the banking facilities were owned by local businessmen and the deposits weren't insured to protect the depositor if a bank failed.

For some families, like ours, the Depression had little effect on social and economic values, as we had been living in an economic depressed state all of our lives. As the outlook on the economic prospects remained somewhat bleak, it was customarily for young persons to remain at home for some time after reaching adulthood. Thus, the cultural, familial, and economic structure of society in general was molded by the depressed era of that day.

Fifteen Kids
and
an Old Blind Horse

The decade of the forties began with the Depression on the wane, but war clouds were looming on the horizon, and America was to enter into one of the most tumultuous periods of its history. While the war gave the country a boost toward economic recovery, it was also an event that changed the social fabric of America that is with us to this day.

This is a humble story of our everyday life as we remember it. It isn't a life that one would desire to return to, but it did have a strange way of helping youngsters find a semblance of responsibility that would have a profound effect on their adult lives.

Hopefully, readers whose daily lives have little in common with the contents herein will better appreciate how their progenitors struggled to survive during the first half of the twentieth century. The following excerpts are presented as an attempt to depict nearly one hundred years of rural life that four generations of the McElhaneys encountered on their little hill farm in northern Morgan Township, Scioto County, Ohio.

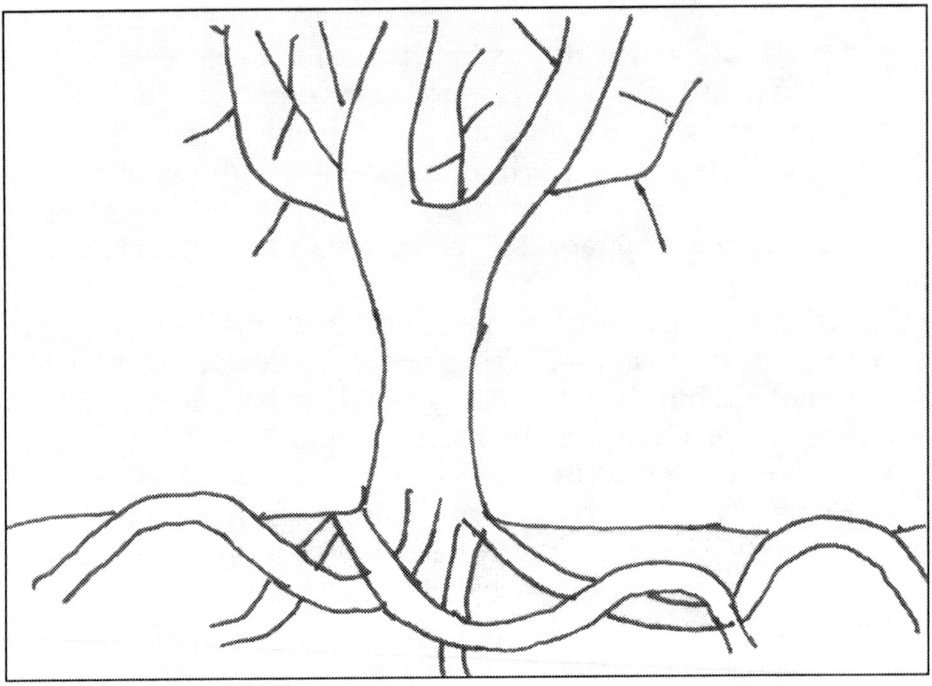

1. Roots

As the rays of the morning sun peeked through the branches of the large oak trees gracing the three high hills to the east of the homestead, activities came to life on the little hill farm where the Robert McElhaney family settled following his discharge from the Civil War in the mid-1860s. All indications led us to believe Robert, our great-grandfather, born in Pennsylvania in 1828 and migrating to Ohio about 1860, lived on upper Camp Creek in southern Pike County, and was raising a family of five young children. In the fall of 1864, Robert suddenly left his family and joined the Union Army at the age of 36 and was involved in military engagements from Tennessee to North Carolina before the Civil War ended.

Official records in Portsmouth, the governing seat of Scioto County, reveal that Robert, who at that time was living in western Morgan Township, had just a few days before his enlistment acquired a track of land consisting of one hundred thirty acres that lay in a hilly and heavily wooded area in northern Morgan Township, about a mile west of the Scioto River. During the Civil War, many people could and did bypass the military service by hiring a surrogate. Robert, being too old for the draft and having a large family at that time, was a perfect candidate to serve as a substitute for one who had means to take advantage of this practice and escape the military service. Whether he acquired the homestead by acting as a surrogate for the previous landowner, we will never know. Following his discharge, Robert moved his family into this backwoods country that would have an impact in determining the destiny of the next four generations.

The National Road, stretching from the eastern side of the Appalachian Mountains to the heart of Illinois, was a main artery for emigrants who desired to find new homes on the western frontier. Sometime during the early 1800s, two families, the Walls and the McElhaneys, of English and Irish descent, were among the many thousands of emigrants who fled the lowlands along the Atlantic Piedmont to find new opportunities in the land beyond the mountains. While the National Road continued to be crowded with pioneers seeking a new life and new opportunities, many left this dusty trail near the village of Pittsburgh, Pennsylvania. To ease the burden of travel, they built boats and wooden rafts and traveled west on the great Ohio River that meandered through the western foothills of the Appalachians, before turning south and west in an attempt to find land located in the Northwest Territory and beyond.

Many emigrants built their new homes along this great river, especially where major tributaries joined the mighty Ohio, and founded cities that are today's landmarks of those hardy forerunners. Cincinnati, a major settlement on the western frontier, offered diversity for homesteading as well as arteries that led to vast regions on the western frontier.

As pioneers rushed across the mountains to settle the rich farmland on the western plains, it was believed by many of that time that God was ushering in a new era of prosperity for this nation, a philosophy referred to by leading proponents of territorial expansion as Manifest Destiny.

The Walls families, probably of English descent, were likely to have been some of the earlier travelers on the National Road, entering Ohio at the beginning of the nineteenth century and settled among the rolling hills of northern Scioto County, Ohio, where they built their homes and chose agriculture as a way of life. Some members of the Walls clan were involved in local government and no doubt had some influence with the establishment of schools, local courts, welfare, and road building. The clan has an ancestral history that remains in that community to this day.

The McElhaney clan departed the National Road in 1855 and followed the Ohio River southwest, settling for some time in Virginia (today's West Virginia), where at least two members of the clan were born. Robert McElhaney, born in Virginia in 1857, was to become the grandfather of the last generation that lived on the homestead. Soon thereafter, the family continued down the Ohio River for another one hundred miles, and at Portsmouth journeyed north on or along the Scioto River for about fifteen miles before leaving the river valley and homesteading on upper Sedan in western Morgan

Township, in the vicinity where the Walls family had already taken root.

The other two families paramount in the McElhaney genealogy were the Salyers and Ealeys. The Salyers were people from France and members of the Huguenot religious movement that fled to America to escape the religious extermination of their society. The Salyers family arrived in or around the area of Charleston, South Carolina, at the beginning of the eighteenth century, and eventually emigrated north through North Carolina, Virginia, and finally to eastern Kentucky, where they nestled in a valley of the great eastern coal fields, known today as Magoffin County. The county seat of Magoffin County is Salyersville, and was named in honor of Samuel Salyers, who served in the Kentucky state legislature and had considerable influence in the formation of the above-mentioned county.

The Ealey family is believed to have had its origins in England and entered the United States probably in Virginia before emigrating northwest to Johnson County, which was adjacent to Magoffin County, in Eastern Kentucky. Our great-grandfather, William Ealey, was born in eastern Kentucky, and at the age of sixteen became a member of the Union Army, serving well over a year before being mustered out of service.

Our maternal grandmother, Mary Ann Salyers, married Daniel Ealey, the son of William, and having been befriended by a member of the Roberts clan, emigrated to Ohio and lived along lower Bear Creek, located in Morgan Township, Scioto County. There, in the year 1916, Myrtle Ealey, their oldest daughter, was married to our father, George McElhaney. They settled on the hill and built a primitive house just a few yards west of our grandparents' home and became the progenitors of the last generation that lived on the McElhaney homestead.

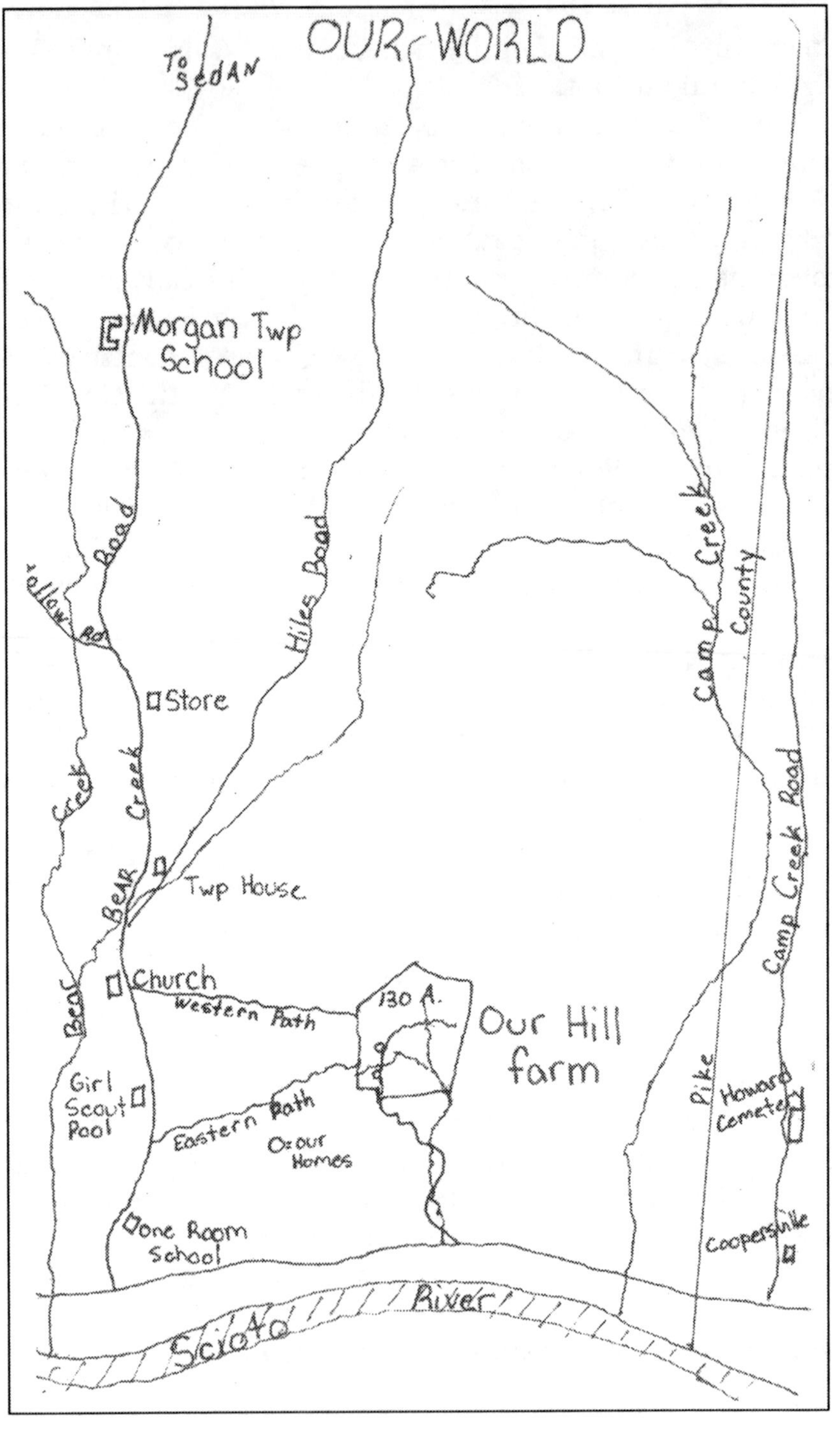

OUR WORLD
To Sedan
Morgan Twp School
Road
Yellow Rd
Hiles Road
Store
Bear Creek
Creek
Twp House
Church
Western Path
Bear
130 A.
Our Hill farm
Girl Scout Pool
Eastern Path
O: our Homes
One Room School
Camp Creek
County
Pike
Camp Creek Road
Howard Cemetery
Coopersville
Scioto River

2. The Hill

Robert McElhaney received title to this hill country in 1864, and following the Civil War settled on a land that would have far-reaching significance for the offspring of the next three generations. Title of the property passed through at least three generations, and those who received the title lived on and worked the land until the next generation took over. The last inhabitants lived on the land until it was abandoned in 1951, and the farm was later sold to the state of Ohio.

The "Hill" consisted of one hundred thirty acres located between two large creeks, Bear Creek to the south and Camp Creek to the north, that partially drained several square miles of land bordering the Scioto River on the west. The property was accessible by a crude road that was forged through a flat wooded area, barely wide enough for a team and wagon, paralleling and crossing a creek three times that occasionally flooded after hard rains. A large mulberry tree that guarded the road on the flat bore luscious and abundant fruit in midsummer and provided a tasty treat for those of us who had an occasion to pass by her when the fruit was ripe. Thereafter, the road meandered up steep slopes and over mud flats under a canopy of large birch, oak, chestnut, walnut, and other deciduous trees for nearly a mile before ascending to the plateau where the farm lay, revealing a serene and picturesque setting for those who had finally reached their destination. At this point, with the Scioto River Valley behind, it was just a few yards from the original dwelling where the clan began.

Two large ranges of hills, one to the east with three distinct peaks and the other to the west, were the principal identifying landmarks. Toward the south, the farm was accessible by two paths, each over a mile long and barely wide enough for a person to walk. These paths provided a walking route to the Bear Creek area through a densely wooded forest, punctuated with old barbed wire fences, a few valleys, small creeks, and fallen trees that obstructed the pathway. The eastern path that ended at the lower Bear Creek road provided a shortcut to the one-room schoolhouse where the older family members attended school. It was also at this juncture that we met the peddler about once a week and traded a few eggs or a chicken or two for a few kitchen staples. The Girl Scout swimming pool, a private and restricted facility, was located nearby, which afforded recreational swimming for us daring lads during the hot summer evenings.

The western path, barely identifiable where it lay against steep bluffs, meandered over rough terrain and through heavily wooded areas and exited on upper Bear Creek near the church, the township house, and a country grocery store. The western part of the farm consisted of rough terrain that was heavily wooded with species of oak, poplar, and a variety of other trees. Some smaller areas were grown up with a variety of small saplings and scrub brush, giving evidence that the land had previously been cleared and used for farming. Following a trail up a steep bluff, one would arrive at the summit of the western range of hills where, years before, a small acreage of land had been cleared of trees and underbrush and used for farming. Nearby was a swampy area which we referred to as the salt lick or bear wallow, an unusual swampy area located on a high plateau of that range of hills.

Following a ridge path toward the west, one would reach the point, a small field that had been cleared years ago for farming. This field was surrounded with medium-sized trees that shaded a large portion of the ground, making it less than optimally productive. To the north from that point the area was heavily wooded and rough. It was called the cove, and was very inhospitable for anything except to provide a sanctuary for the animals of the forest.

After returning to the site of our dwellings, one can observe the only road on the farm, which meandered in a northerly direction from our house, bordering small streams and scrubby fruit trees along a land that had once been cleared for farming and later abandoned, and a corn patch, before it began its circuitous route through the woods for several hundred feet, exiting at a clearing containing two or three acres of flat land, which we referred to as the Leeper Field, the mainstay of our agricultural enterprise. The farm seldom had more than ten to fifteen acres of cleared land at any time, and a large portion of the land that surrounded our homes and gardens was used as pasture land for the animals.

An area along the eastern ridge of the farm large enough to build the original house and utility buildings was prepared by moving soil and rock to the lower side to make a reasonably level spot for the buildings. A small cellar was dug by hand before it was walled with large stones and used to store vegetables and canned goods. After the house was finished, the main floor consisted of a covered porch, a rather large kitchen for that day, a living room, and a bedroom. There was an unfinished attic where, presumably, some of the children slept. A small fireplace, supporting a rather large chimney for that day, was the centerpiece of the living room and an old grandfather clock graced its mantle. During the summer evenings, the occupants in the living room were often serenaded by the twittering and fluttering chimney swallows as they flitted to their nests for the night. A tar paper roof kept the structure dry, but its very nature required yearly maintenance to prevent leaking.

A smokehouse/utility storage building stood at the southeastern corner of the yard, and a large dug well lay off to the northeast side near the porch. A chicken house was a necessity for all rural residents of that period in time, and Grandma's was positioned below the house at the western corner of the yard. The barn and corn crib were structured along the road just west of the dwelling.

Various fruit trees were planted along the bank below the house, and we all fondly remember the grape arbor and plum and apple trees, and principally the quince tree that bore a yellow apple-like fruit, somewhat flattened or pear-shaped. It was most inedible in the raw state, but when cooked it could be used in flavoring preserves or added to cooked apples to give flavor and tartness. A few rose bushes graced the side yard, while the catalpa and cedar trees provided shade during hot summer afternoons. A large oak tree guarded the other corner of the house on the west.

Adjacent to the dwellings was a semi-level plot of ground that our grandparents used for a garden which was fenced to protect the precious produce from the domestic animals that grazed nearby. Generally, wire fences would circumference dwelling structures and gardens of that day to keep the animals at a safe distance.

The homestead was located on the western side of a range of hills, and during the winter months the sun rose very late, casting long, cold shadows over the land before bringing warmth at midmorning. Likewise, the western range was quite high, and ushered in an early sunset, leaving the little valley in an extended period of twilight, making for long and cold winter nights but giving relief from the hot afternoons with cooler evenings during the summer months.

The McElhaneys moved to the hill farm in mid-1860, and it has never been determined whether or not the main structure existed when they arrived, but other structures had to be built, wells dug, and land cleared for gardens and farming. Stories have surfaced to substantiate that several of Robert's brothers were among the clan when they first arrived. Robert, our great-grandfather, who was the apparent owner of the farm, was barely settled and had gotten a good start on the building program when he died in 1875 at the age of forty-seven years, after living on his farm for only ten years. At the time of his death, there were nine children living, and twins would be born just a few months hence. His absence left the children in dire straits, and life was very difficult for the clan without their father. Their mother died in 1886, leaving the children to fend for themselves.

In the early 1890s, Congress passed the Military Pension Act to provide assistance for needy survivors of Civil War veterans. An examination of Robert's military pension records reveals that the entire clan was living in acute poverty. These records contain sworn affidavits from representatives of the local government and other leading citizens concerning the family's living conditions and the perilous consequences of delayed assistance. It was at this time that our grandfather, Robert McElhaney, moved his family to the hill, possibly to provide leadership and stability to his younger siblings. How they all got along in that three-roomed dwelling is a mystery that was never revealed. Our father, George, was one of the children, and he was to live most of his life on the hill.

A second house was constructed just west of the original house by our parents following their marriage in 1916. As far as anyone knows, there are no existing photographs of our home, but it was depicted in a painting by our nephew several years ago from a description given to him by his mother. The foundation for the house consisted of large flat rocks that were placed at various intervals to support the floor joists. It was a simple configuration of a dwelling, emphasizing a living/master bedroom combination which served as the main room of the house. The furnishings included a couple of chairs, a stand to hold a coal oil lamp, a bed, and a dresser with a mirror. At one time, our older brothers brought home an old Victrola talking machine, to the chagrin of our parents, to play records. This talking machine was an up-to-date musical entertainment center of that day, even though it was powered by a coiled spring that required winding after each record was played.

Abutting the living room on the north was the other bedroom large enough for two beds and a pallet or so. The mattress covers were made of a heavy cloth material, probably from feed sacks, and were filled with padding that consisted of straw, grass, or leaves. The pillow covers were simply smaller and were made from the same material. Sometimes the pillows were filled with feathers. A chest for clothing rounded out the bedroom furniture. A square opening in the bedroom ceiling revealed the loft, the space between the ceiling and the roof that was used for storage, but it was much too small for sleeping quarters.

Our dwelling was heated with a Sears & Roebuck tin stove that had no shields for protection, and all of us children have seen its pregnant sides become so hot that it glowed brilliantly in the dimly lighted room. The flue would often get so hot that it would have a red glow between the stove and the ceiling. During the coldest weather periods, the stove didn't have the capacity to keep the rooms warm, no matter how much wood we fed it.

The kitchen, a build-on after the family grew larger, was structured against the west side of the house. An old cookstove adorned the kitchen and was used for cooking and baking. As we cooked our meals, we also heated water in a built-in reservoir that was located adjacent to the fire box. Near the stove was a wooden box that had to be replenished daily with firewood and kindling, the necessary items to make a fire to cook the next meal. The kitchen stove was the only source of heat for that room, and during the winter months our meals were consumed very quickly, as the old cooking stove wasn't very efficient for space heating. Since we didn't fire the cookstove during the night, the kitchen area would become very cold overnight, and quite often we would have to break ice in the wash pan before we could wash our faces. A large homemade family table rounded out the kitchen furniture. (It has often been asked why some of us children were much taller than others in the family, and the reply was that the house was built to the contour of the ground and the lucky ones sat on the low side of the table and the food naturally gravitated to that position.) Alongside the wall was an old cupboard for storing cooking utensils.

A couple of coal oil lamps provided light for our house and could be carried from room to room when needed. However, the light from the lamps was often so faint that a passerby would need to look a second time to detect any illumination that was being emitted from any of the three windows.

The four entrance/exit doors of the house offered ample passage and safety. At one period in time in 1935, there would have been up to eleven persons living in this simple three-room dwelling. A patio was structured on the north side of the kitchen where one could rest from the labors of the day. During the summer evenings, we were entertained with the flight of the chimney birds as they darted back and forth in the twilight, snatching mosquitoes and other insects from the air for their evening meal. Most summer evenings we enjoyed the musical performances of the whippoorwill and other feathery creatures before they called it a day. The noisy crickets were the last to perform each evening, indicating that the daylight hours were coming to an end.

A flat rock sidewalk led from the kitchen door to the old smokehouse that was located just south of the dwelling. The smokehouse was a multipurpose building, used for storing our few tools and other miscellaneous items, but its main purpose was for smoking meat after we had butchered a hog. A small wood-burning stove, without a chimney, was fired with green hickory logs, and many a spring morning one could observe hickory smoke wisping from the cracks and the ceiling of the smokehouse following butchering season.

The yard was enclosed with a fence and graced by a couple of rose bushes, two large oak trees, and a flat rock sidewalk that led to the front door. Within the yard were a variety of domestic fruit trees, including apple, cherry and peach, along with a grape arbor. The yard itself was manicured with a sickle, swung by hand, of course.

An old grindstone was stationed beside a large oak tree located to the west of the house and was used for sharpening heavy tools, such as axes. It required two persons to operate this machine, one to hold the implement to be sharpened, and one to pour water on the stone to enhance the sharpening process. Generally, the younger helper's job was to carry the water and pour it on the stone while turning the handle.

Another important building for the comfort of the family was the outhouse, located near the edge of the creek about a hundred feet across the little road. It was no place to loaf in cold weather! This was the only structure on the property that had water under pressure, and only when the occupant had an acute case of urgency. First priority went to the oldest and the most influential, and seldom would their relief period be challenged. All were appreciative of the Sears & Roebuck's catalogue, which served two purposes. Those old catalogues kept us up-to-date on all the latest clothing and household fashions, giving us something to dream about, and their worn pages prevented many stains on the finger! If all the pages of the catalogue had been used, one might revert to pieces of a brown grocery bag or, as a last resort, a corncob.

(Many rural families would have buckets or "slop jars" for nocturnal relief, rather than brace the cold weather during the small hours of the night. Hopefully, it would have been removed before the breakfast hour to prevent the permeating of opposing odors!)

Between the house and the outhouse was the scene

where many conflicts surfaced among the siblings of our family. This area was known as the wood yard, and we will reconnect with that subject shortly. Adjacent to the wood yard was the hen house that provided an important source of our food supply, mostly with eggs, but occasionally with meat.

The family garden was just to the south of the old smokehouse, where a large variety of vegetables were grown to provide the bulk of our winter's food. It was also the home of a large gooseberry bush, whose fruit, like the quince, would readily make one's lips pucker when it was stolen before it was ripe. Waiting for its ripening was rewarding but seldom did all the berries make it to maturity. An old-fashioned peach tree was its nearby companion and provided tasty morsels in early autumn.

The last important landmark to be identified was a fenced field south of the garden called the potato patch. This was a rather large area to be allotted for growing potatoes, but its size was necessary as the soil, severely lacking in nutrients, didn't overproduce for the family needs.

This primitive setting was the home of fifteen children who were born into our family in a span of about twenty-one years during the early decades of the twentieth century.

3. The Necessities of Life

Aside from the physical aspects of the homestead, there were basic necessities for everyday survival. These included water, food, fuel, and clothing.

The endeavor to find a water supply in rural regions was a continuing problem. We couldn't rely on small creek reservoirs, as they were mostly dry excepting a short period following rain, and cisterns were not reliable for an adequate water supply during long and dry summer months, as many frontier cisterns were not properly sealed and were likely to allow the water to leach into the abutting soil. Frequent rainfall was necessary to maintain a reserve for home and animal consumption. The better solution was to dig enough wells to maintain an adequate supply of water.

The first step taken in preparation to dig a well was to find as many flat rocks as needed, nearly a foot square and three or four inches thick. Rocks were numerous on most hill farms, and were brought to the surface during the winter's freezing and thawing period and must be removed before spring plowing. In this removal, they were hauled to the edge of the fields and dumped, but in some cases were used to build or reinforce fence lines. Rocks could also be found in nearby creeks where storm water had unearthed those that were close to the surface of the ground. The selected rocks were hauled to the site where the well was to be dug.

Before digging began, a source of underground water must be determined. At least one member in most frontier families possessed mystical powers to "witch" a well. Most often, a nice forked branch from a peach tree having two equal-sized extremities was used by the "witcher" to determine the exact spot to dig the well. The witcher would walk back and forth over a predetermined spot of ground, holding the witching branch tightly with both hands while keeping the point of the branch parallel with the ground. When the fork of the branch pointed toward the ground, it was determined that the witcher had discovered an underground vein of water, and that spot would be marked with a stake. Several more passes would be made to make sure the reading was correct before the digging began, but this digging process was no easy chore. Working in a hole five or six feet in diameter and up to fifteen feet deep became a long and drawn-out process. Buckets tethered with ropes would be filled with dirt and hoisted to the top of the ground with a windlass, but most likely drawn by hand. The dirt would be scattered nearby or hauled from the site to be used for other purposes. Following several days of hard work, and having finished removing the dirt, a layer of rock would be placed tightly on the bottom of the well. Having finished the foundation, layers of rocks were put in place until the walls were laid up. Finally, the jagged edges would be trimmed to make the finished sides somewhat uniform, and when completed, a covering of some sort would be placed over its top.

Having finished the well, we could do nothing but wait and hope for it to fill up with water, but the best of those dug wells could only produce surface water that leached into its basin. It was thought that locating the well as close as possible to a creek might enhance the chances of having a more productive supply of water. There were five such wells on the property, and together they hardly produced enough water for the family to use. Many wells were not very productive because they could not be dug deep enough by hand to strike an underground vein of water.

All water for household use had to be drawn from the wells in a bucket and carried into the house. The well to the south, a favorite one beyond our property line, was nearly a thousand feet away, and several trips to the well in one day made the water bearer appreciate dinner that evening. The wells provided another important function, especially during hot summer months. Any perishable foods, such as dairy products, would be placed in a container and lowered into the well, just above the water line. Pioneer refrigeration!

When a well stopped producing, it was time to clean it out, as the adjacent soil would likely be silting into the rock wall and preventing the ground water from entering into it. Two of our wells were judged unsafe for consumption, probably by the way the water smelled. We didn't have access to simple household chemicals to disinfect them; therefore, these two were practically useless for cooking and drinking. The three remaining wells barely produced ample water for our meager needs during the dry summer months, and it was a constant struggle to get enough water for our household use and provide water for the few animals we owned. In most small creeks, shallow holes are washed out by spring rains, and we relied on this source of water supply for the animals until the water holes dried up. In extreme dry periods, we had to lead some of the animals far down the creek to find a water hole.

The garden was of immense importance, as it was our main source of food supply. It also required constant work, as we believed the vegetables needed to be cultivated weekly. We children were responsible for pulling weeds and keeping the garden in an orderly manner.

An abundant variety of vegetable seeds and plants were planted each spring for our summer fare and winter canning. Favorite veggies were pole beans, sweet peas, and tomatoes. Beans were planted in hills about three feet apart, and when the vines started to show vigorous growth, we would cut small hickory poles about seven or eight feet long, sharpen the larger ends, and shove them into the ground next to the plants. When they were tied at the top, the structure resembled a teepee. The vines would quickly grow to the top, producing protruding foliage and bountiful fruit. This was an effective method of producing an abundance of beans, and we generally feasted throughout the late summer months and still had plenty for canning.

We canned the green beans in half-gallon jars, and when a determined number had been prepared for the winter, the remaining crop would be allowed to grow to maturity. While the beans still contained some moisture, they would be picked and shelled. We preserved the mature beans by using a needle and thread to string each bean on a line before hanging them on nails in the attic to dry. Good soup beans for a cold winter night!

Sweet peas, an early spring vegetable, were planted for immediate table consumption. They were cooked and served like green beans, but they did not keep well when we attempted to preserve them.

We grew the old-fashioned tomatoes that made an excellent table dish when eaten raw, and it was important that we canned large quantities of this vegetable, as it was a main staple in our diet.

When vegetables reached maturity, all hands were busy in preparation for canning. The jars were thoroughly cleansed by boiling them in hot water before they were filled with the fruit or vegetable to be canned. After the lids had been tightened, the jars were placed into a tub of water that had been heated over a roaring outdoor fire. After being boiled for an hour or so we removed the jars, and when they had cooled, hopefully the jar lids would have sealed and preserved the contents. This pioneer's method of preservation was referred to as "cold packing," and it worked well before the pressure canner became popular.

Not all vegetables were canned. When cucumbers grew to a respectable size, they would be pickled by placing them in an old stone crock filled with salt/vinegar brine and marinating them throughout the summer and fall. Come midwinter, these cucumbers were a welcome addition to our meals.

Digging and storing potatoes was always a big job. Regardless of our effort, it was most difficult to control the weeds, and at digging time the potato field would resemble a big weed patch. After mowing the weeds with a scythe and clearing them from the potato patch, a horse pulling a twelve-inch shovel plow would roll the potatoes to the top of the ground, where they could be picked up and spread on a dry surface. In a day or so, we stored them in the potato bin, located in the cellar at Grandma's house. Hopefully, we would have an ample supply for the winter, with seed potatoes left over for next year's planting.

In July, the corn patch would be surveyed to determine if the ears were in the milk stage. If it was determined that the corn was ready, several ears would be husked and cleaned, and cut from the cob to be cooked with other vegetables. Often, they were boiled in water and eaten as "roasting ears." Though our corn was of the field variety, we looked forward to the short season when we could have fresh corn to eat.

Some vegetables matured early in the summer, such as peas, lettuce and onions, and after they had been gathered, a small area where they had grown would be cleared of weeds, and after the ground had been spaded, turnip seed was sown for an autumn vegetable, to be either eaten raw or cooked.

Throughout the summer, every three days or so, we each grabbed a gallon bucket (syrup can) and headed to the berry patch. Struggling through the briars to pluck the berries from the vines in shorts, and barefooted, made one wish there was an ole swimming hole nearby. Occasionally, we exited the berry patch on the run when someone got excited about seeing a snake slithering among the vines. That evening, Dad would assure us that the snake was harmless and the berries would be picked on the morrow!

After the picking was completed and we had soothed our many briar scratches with cool water and/or any kind of cream available, generally lard, we were often rewarded with a blackberry cobbler at the evening meal, but not before the day's picking was separated from the debris and washed in preparation for cold packing. Following this preparation, they were kept in a cool place until the next day when they were to be canned. The last chore was to carry them to Grandma's cellar to be stored for winter.

Occasionally, the berries would be mashed and, after adding a little sugar, were cooked until the solution became a semisolid state. When the mix was suitable, it would be poured into jars. After it had cooled, a hot liquid paraffin base was used to seal the jars and preserve the contents. During the cold winter, those luscious berries and jams were some treat to the palate, and all scratches received during the picking season would have long been forgotten!

The several fruit trees that dotted the landscape received considerable attention. When the marble-sized tart fruit of the gnarly crab apple tree was eaten in an uncooked state, any excess consumption would, in a very short time, stimulate an urgency to scamper to the outhouse and make a run on the pages of the Sears & Roebuck catalogue! Seldom did any of the fruit over ripen, as we were most anxious to indulge as soon as it was edible. Any fruit that survived the family raiders would be picked and cooked for breakfast. Cooked fruit at our house was generally referred to as dessert.

Not all food found in trees was native. We were always scanning the older trees in an attempt to find holes that may have indicated the activity of a beehive. When we did find a tree with the prospect of a beehive, and if we detected any activity, it lost its good standing before the passing of too many nights. After felling the bee tree, a coal oil torch was used to smoke the bees, which would kill many of them and tended to drive the others away before an attempt was made to take the honey. When we believed the bees to be subdued, making it safe to approach the hive, a large notch would be cut from the tree near the hive opening, affording entrance to the luscious honey inside. An older and large beehive might yield several pails of honey.

We children looked forward to harvesting these beehives, not just for the honey, but for the honeycomb, which was a good source of chewing gum! For other chewing gum, we improvised when the occasion presented itself. During the summer when we were working in the wheat field for a nearby farmer, a handful of wheat grains, after being chewed, would become a gummy substance akin to processed chewing gum, although it lacked the sweet flavor. A pocket full of wheat grains would keep one in chewing gum for several days! When we canned jams and jellies, paraffin wax was used to seal the jars, and any left over was used for chewing gum. Our best source of chewing gum came from the slippery elm tree. After the outer bark had been removed, the soft juicy layer of pulp found next to the trunk was chewy, and one could grind on this gummy substance all afternoon.

Most people living in a country setting raised chickens, and it required a considerable number of them to supply a large family with eggs and meat. It wasn't unusual to have a half dozen old hens nesting, and three to four weeks later see one surface with ten to twelve little fluffy chicks. At one time we owned a small incubator, and raised our own chicks by placing three or four dozen fertile eggs into the incubator in early spring, keeping them warm with a kerosene lamp and turning each egg every twenty-four hours. We would hope to be greeted with a lively flock of chicks in about three weeks!

Nearly every spring, when we were without the incubator and didn't have nesting hens, we ordered one hundred day-old chicks, about half male and half female, again from Sears & Roebuck. The chicks required constant care for the first couple weeks but grew quickly, and it wasn't long until they could be turned out in the chicken yard. However, there were chicken hawks living in the nearby woods, and occasionally one would swoop down and grab a small chick for its own lunch. We learned early on to guard the chicks by keeping Dad's old rifle at hand, and upon spotting a predator fire a few shots to ward off any aggression toward a noon meal.

Corn was a good source of feed for chickens and one of our daily chores would be to shell enough corn to feed them. It wasn't so difficult to remove the grains from the cob if an ear of corn was held in one hand while taking a corn cob in the other and rubbing the grains vigorously at an angle. Later on, we acquired a contraption that was cranked by hand and would shell a whole ear of corn at a time. With us keeping plenty of food before the young chicks, we were assured that the males would mature into fryers by early summer. Not only did the young roosters make good fryers, they were as faithful as an alarm clock, awakening the residents well before daybreak each morning.

The pullets, hopefully, would begin to lay eggs before winter as much of our diet was from this source, and our income was generated by selling eggs to the local grocer. It was important that a few eggs survive our kitchen table to exchange for other necessities of the home. Occasionally, instead of visiting the grocery store, we met the peddler along the Bear Creek road and bartered eggs for such staples as sugar, flour, and salt. When an old hen became too old to lay eggs, it was customary to plan a chicken and dumpling dinner for the Sunday fare.

Siblings our age, regardless of the environment, were natural rivals. We were always trying to get the upper hand on each other to show who was boss, but blood was seldom shed in our disputes. The bloodiest place on the farm took place just a few yards from our house where the "hanging tree" stood. The hanging tree was a portly elm tree having a large branch protruding horizontally from its trunk, about ten feet high, and was suitable for a hanging that hopefully occurred at least once a year.

Sometime in early spring, we would barter for or buy one or two weaned pigs from a nearby farmer or neighbor. As young pigs were very difficult to handle without crates, we solved the problem by placing them in feed sacks, which helped to keep them under control until they had been released in the pig pen. The pig pen was enclosed with an old woven wire fence and those pigs were forever escaping, especially while they were small, and we children were constantly running after them. We learned the importance of checking the fence and repairing the holes before the pigs escaped!

Barnyard manure, in our situation, was our only source of garden fertilizer. It was also the source of many weeds, and pigs like fresh green foliage. We youngsters were responsible for pulling weeds in the garden and carrying them to the pig pen. One variety of hay we raised was a clover called Lespedeza. Periodically, we would take the hand sickle and cut an armful of this clover and feed it to the pigs. In late autumn, acorns from the oak trees that grew nearby would begin to fall to the ground, and they became another source of hog feed. Gathering a bucket of acorns from the ground was no small chore!

When a pig began to mature, by nature, it would root up the ground with its nose and tear up the pig pen. To prevent this destruction, three or four ringers was clamped through the upper portion of its snout, making its nose quite tender, but it ended the rooting activity, at least until its nose healed. If we had a good year, there would be a hog or two to butcher, and sometime during the winter months, we would be rewarded with a supply of fresh meat for the tender care we had provided in rearing those pigs.

In preparation for butchering day, an outdoor fire was started near the butchering station, and several gallons of water would be poured into a large wash tub and heated until it came to a boil. This boiling water was then ready to be poured over the carcass, a process we referred to as "scalding the hog." As daylight approached, the quarry was killed with one well-placed rifle shot in the middle of the forehead. Very quickly, we used a sharp knife to stick the hog in the neck, severing the juggler vein, so that it would bleed thoroughly. The carcass would then be placed on the sled and dragged to the butchering station. Large feed sacks were spread over the carcass to preserve the heat when hot water was poured over its exterior in an attempt to loosen the hair, which was subsequently scraped off.

Having cleansed the hair from its body, a slit in the flesh at the back of the lower hind legs would be made to expose the tendons. The tendons were then stretched over a gambrel, a strong pole that was notched at each end to hold the tendons in place. These notches prevented the carcass from sliding off and dropping the fare to the ground. The gambrel was tied to a rope that had been thrown over the hanging limb, and the carcass was hoisted into the air where it could more easily be dressed.

Very little of the hog was wasted. Internal organs, such as the heart, liver, and the lights, were consumed. The edible meat of the head was extracted and ground into a loaf, called head cheese, not the most tasty part of the hog. The tongue was never a favorite dish and some objections were audible when it was placed on the table, but in the end, most plates were bare when they were ready to be put in the dish pan for washing. The feet were sometimes pickled in salt/vinegar brine, but this item wasn't a favorite morsel at our house. The fat near the belly was "rendered" in an old iron kettle and poured into the lard can where it cooled and solidified.

Lard does not spoil easily and can usually be stored at room temperature throughout the year and used in cooking. (In some instances, lard would be used for axle grease, but beef tallow, when it was available, was a better source of lubricant!) The solids, leftovers from this process called "cracklings," were nothing more than fatty flesh that was still clinging to the hide after the lard had been released by boiling. These cracklings were stored in a container to dry, and when they became crisp, we enjoyed French fries well before the potato made that term famous.

A portion of the lean meat was ground into sausage, and when fried, it provided a savory meal that was relished by all of us. The grease left in the skillet after frying sausage was a favorite when one took a biscuit and soaked it in the sausage grease before eating. Sometimes, thick cream from the milk pail would be mixed with the grease to enrich the taste. This mixture was referred to as "sop," and was believed to have been Dad's favorite dish.

Should any of the hams, shoulders, or bacon slabs survive the winter, they were hung from the ceiling of the smokehouse and smoked with a smoldering hickory fire for about six weeks. They were then scored and filled with salt to preserve the meat until it was consumed.

It was of primary importance to have a milk cow for our dairy needs. When the cow became fresh—that is, gave birth to a calf—we generally had ample milk for the family for a period of about ten months until she went dry again. If she gave birth to a bull calf, we might be fortunate to sell it and buy staples for the home. Seldom was a beef butchered, as we were unable to manage that much meat at one time as we never canned beef, and the few dollars we received for selling the steer were very important in the purchasing of family necessities.

Earlier generations used the bull calves as working oxen, but oxen are slower workers than horses or mules, more temperamental, and much more difficult to handle. When an ox became too temperamental to handle the usual way, a ring would be clamped into the tender membrane located between his nostrils, making it much easier to control him. Heifer calves were prized more than the bull calves, as they would replace the older cows for our future milk supply.

Any milk that was not consumed immediately would be set aside for a few days until a thick luscious cream rose to the top, and after being skimmed it was used to flavor other foods, such as fruits. When milk was two or three days old, it was churned until butter particles, being lighter than the liquid, rose to the top. After these particles were skimmed, they were formed into a butter ball and used as a biscuit spread or as a seasoning for other foods. The liquid solution left over was called buttermilk. After adding a little salt and pepper, one had a tasty drink! Instead of going through the churning process, we often took a shortcut in processing it. The milk was set aside for three or four days to allow the cream to rise to the top. After the cream had been skimmed to be used to season various fruits and vegetables, the liquid was left in a pail to age, causing the solution to turn into a semisolid state. When this solution was vigorously stirred, and after a good measure of salt and pepper were added, we had a tasty dish called cottage cheese...well, almost! Maybe clabbered milk.

Other than water, milk, or an occasional fruit or

vegetable juice drink, we again relied on the natural resources to add variety to our diet. Small sassafras trees were plentiful at the end of the potato patch, near the west side of the garden, as well as other places on the farm. The aromatic bark of the roots could easily be taken and cleaned for use in preparing a tasty drink. When the bark was immersed in a pan of water and brought to a simmer on the old cookstove, its flavor and color would permeate the water and we would have a beverage we called root beer...er, sassafras tea. Of course, too much of the stuff makes one light-headed and may cause one's nose to bleed!

Having sold our eggs and purchased flour, we could make a variety of breads for the table. An oblong metal baking pan was the mainstay in baking white flour biscuits, cornbread, and occasionally corn cakes, but most frequently pone bread. Pone bread was simply a bread batter that was poured into the baking pan and baked in the oven.

A good dish of sausage gravy helped to make the meal complete. We began by heating sausage grease in the skillet, if there was any in the larder, sifting into the grease several tablespoons of flour, adding a liberal amount of milk, a tablespoon of lard, a pinch of salt, a dash of pepper, and when available, a little sausage meat. After stirring thoroughly, the mixture was cooked to perfection, and everyone enjoyed a good gravy dish to complement the home-baked bread! When we lacked the necessary ingredients for good gravy, we made flour and water gravy, a bland dish that had little nourishment, but it did add bulk in our stomachs.

Light bread was a commercial bakery product that many stores began to carry as a staple, and was becoming available for the more well-to-do folks. We learned to call it "sunshine," as it didn't appear to have as much body to it as homemade bread. Although we made fun of the product and the people who ate it, we later began to understand the only reason for this criticism was the fact that we couldn't afford to buy store bread! We seldom experienced the joy of eating a loaf of bread that was baked in a bakery!

Our dessert often consisted of a piece of pone bread covered with sugar water—a concoction prepared by stirring a good helping of sugar into a pan of hot water and boiling it until the solution began to thicken slightly—often referred to as southern Ohio syrup. When this mixture was topped with a few spoonfuls of cream from the day-old milk, the meal was complete!

Quite often, our Sunday evening meals consisted of a bowl of cooked mush. We just added a liberal helping of milk and ate it while it was hot! Later we might get out the sack of popcorn that was stored in the attic and use an old corn cob to shell a couple of ears, as the tips of popcorn were often quite prickly and could make your hands sore if you attempted to remove the grains without using protection for your hands. We then heated the grains in bacon grease until the noise stopped, and if the majority of the grains popped, it was a success. We would have ample grains left over to grind our teeth on.

When we were visited with winter snows, we made snow cream simply by collecting a pan of snow. We then added a liberal amount of cream, a little vanilla if we had any, a few tablespoons of sugar, and stirred it until the mixture was creamy. Yummy!

During the fall and winter months when ammunition was available, one of us would take to the woods with Dad's old shotgun in an attempt to supplement the family diet with fresh meat. If successful, an occasional rabbit would be the fare of the day, but squirrels were more abundant and we enjoyed a greater degree of success when hunting them. Either was a welcome source of meat for the table, as it would have been a long spell since the previous butchering season. Seldom were the hunting laws observed, but it was our property, and we only hunted wild game for food. We learned early on not to hunt during the animals' reproductive cycles, which occurred during the late winter and spring months.

Our first cousin, who lived on Camp Creek, was a frequent visitor at our home and loved to hunt. His hunting companion, a little white-and-brown spotted dog named Bounce, was very good at treeing squirrels. On one particular hunt, Bounce apparently treed a squirrel, but after scanning the tree from all sides, we were unable to spot the squirrel. Bounce wouldn't give up. We finally spotted a hole in the upper portion of the trunk—a natural phenomenon that occurs after a tree loses a limb and the pulp dies—that might be a hiding place for the squirrel.

After this discovery, we decided that Bounce was right and the squirrel was hiding in the tree. Not desiring to lose the hunt or to go without a tasty dish for supper, we were determined to fell the tree and kill the squirrel as it tried to escape. After fetching the saw and axe, it wasn't long until we yelled "timber!" With the shotgun loaded and ready to shoot the escaping squirrel, and in the excitement of the hunt, we failed to hold Bounce until the tree had fallen. As the tree approached its final landing, Bounce was at the scene ready to pounce on the quarry, unaware of the danger he had put himself into. A fun and exciting day in the hunt quickly turned into tragedy. The dream of a sumptuous supper evaporated with the loss of his faithful hunting companion.

Each township in the county had a judicial representative of the courts called a Justice of the Peace, or for short, just Squire, who adjudicated acts of violations if they were not deemed too serious. Another local citizen with the title of constable was appointed to enforce local laws and investigate minor infractions and when necessary, present his findings before the Squire for judgment. Both officers were subject to the county court system. There were also state law enforcement agents called game wardens who enforced the hunting laws of the land.

It was customary for some local hunters to take a squirrel or two before the hunting season began, as the city hunters frequented private property and took advantage of the short hunting season to the chagrin of us country folk. A neighbor, whom we looked upon as a country bully, lived adjacently to the area where our lane intersected the highway, delighted in bragging about beating those city folks in the hunt, and felt he was well ahead of the game when he took a couple of squirrels one afternoon before the hunting season started. However, another person was in the same woods, observing the out-of-season hunting practices of the locals.

The Squire was startled when the warden and the poacher appeared at his door with the expectation that the Squire would adjudicate the offense. After hearing the complaint and the plea, the good Squire assessed a levy of one dollar for each piece of contraband. Not entirely satisfied with the smallness of the assessment but knowing he had to accept the decision, the warden went on his way. The defendant, who knew the Squire personally, stayed on a few moments to chat, and to the Squire's embarrassment, his "housekeeper" rose from her chair, revealing the successful hunt the Squire himself had enjoyed that same afternoon and was in process of dressing his own catch at the time he was interrupted. Without saying, the hunter was a little put out but felt lucky by getting off with the smallness of his fine. Some of us were pleasantly pleased upon hearing that the local bully had finally gotten his comeuppance.

Not all food products were domestic or passed over the kitchen table. It didn't take too many years for a youngster to learn that some foods found in the woods was safe, nourishing, and sometimes even delectable. Various kinds of berries that we didn't preserve were consumed directly from the vine. Dewberries grew on small vines that lay close to the ground, and a variety of huckleberry which resembles a small blueberry made delicious treats when milk and sugar were added—if they did get to the kitchen table. Large patches of huckleberry vines grew on the hill to the east of Grandma's house, but one had to work long and hard to pick enough to make a berry cobbler. When a huckleberry cobbler was set on the table for the evening dessert, we knew the effort we expended to retrieve them was well worth it.

One afternoon while we kids were picking huckleberries, an older brother yelled out that he had been bitten by a snake, but we put him off thinking he was just crying wolf, an act that we all had been guilty of at times, although we had occasionally seen snakes on that hillside. Well, it didn't take long for his leg to start swelling and the berry picking ended with all of us scampering to the house. As the afternoon wore on, it was imperative that he received medical assistance, and that evening when Dad came home, arrangements were made to take him to a doctor for treatment. We all believed he was bitten by a copperhead, a small poisonous reptile that lived in protected places like the huckleberry patch, whose bite was quite painful but generally not life threatening if it was treated in time. He really had it easy around the house for the next couple of weeks!

Following late spring rains, certain white oak trees yielded small bulbs about the size of a golf ball, and if picked and eaten immediately, they were quite tasty. The hard part was shinning up the tree and climbing out on a limb to pick this tasty morsel.

Most rural people have heard of and probably can recognize the mayapple, a small flowering plant that grows in the woods and bears a yellow pulp-like fruit that is edible when ripened. Few people knew the fruit was good to eat. We did!

The papaw, a tree similar in size to an apple tree, yielded a yellow mushy fruit that had a taste of its own. Although this fruit was safe to eat, it took just a few visits to the papaw tree to get a bellyful that lasted the rest of the year.

Wild grapes were plentiful and would reach maturity after a heavy frost or two in autumn. Sometimes the vines were entwined along an old tree trunk that had fallen, and the grapes were easily picked, but when they were twisted around a standing tree, well, we would just have to climb the tree to obtain the fruit!

The persimmon, when ripened, is a small orange/reddish fruit that grows on a tree about the size of an apple tree, and it is one species that none of us children raided before the fruit reached maturity, which generally occurred after several frosts in the fall.

Wild nuts of several varieties, including walnuts and chestnuts, were good sources of winter treats and were harvested in late fall or early winter and stored in the attic for cold weather goodies. It was believed that eating walnuts before they were thoroughly dried, or about midwinter, would cause one to become inflicted with painful boils and sores.

Our clan seldom enjoyed the sport of fishing, mainly

because our time and energy were needed for farm work. On a few occasions, however, the older boys would toss a long throw line—a long line with several hooks attached and baited with dough balls—into the Scioto River in an attempt to catch catfish. This line need not be attended but once a day. When a catfish was caught, it was generally ill-prepared as we were not very well-acquainted in preparing fish, and we weren't encouraged to pursue this activity.

Springtime was the spawning season for suckers that made their annual run up Camp Creek, a nearby drainage creek just to the north of our property, to nest and lay their eggs.

When the sucker fish grew to adulthood, it would be up to eighteen inches long and weigh a couple of pounds. When spawning, they were tenacious in protecting their spawning bed, an instinct which made them vulnerable to predators. We made a crude fishing outfit by cutting a small branch from a tree to be used as a fishing pole. To this branch we attached one end of a line to the pole and tied treble hooks to the other end of the line. The quarry could easily be snagged as the treble hooks were dragged alongside the fleshy part of the sucker's body. At the height of the spawning season, it would take but a short while to snag enough suckers for a meal. The sucker was a fleshy fish, but there were numerous fine bones throughout its entire body and one had to be very careful not to become choked on a bone when eating this morsel. This fish wasn't safe for children to eat, and we didn't attempt to catch them very often.

The lack of breeding stock contributed greatly to the deficiency of our diet, but our land just wasn't fertile enough to produce the quantity of feed necessary to feed additional animals. Just one boar and a sow would have produced several pigs each year, and instead of having one or two hogs to butcher, we would have had a half dozen or so, which would have greatly enhanced our table needs. Neither could we raise our own working animals, as stallions were difficult to control and could not be trusted, especially around children. To replace or add an additional work horse, we were forced to go on the market in an attempt to acquire one, most always without the necessary resources to go first class.

A distant cousin, who lived on upper Sedan, owned a large black stallion of working class stock and would occasionally ride a circuit, and "serve" the farmers' mares when their owners desired to raise colts from them. The local farmer might send a notice that his mare was "in season," or the breeder would rely on his own records concerning the birth of a previous foal, as to the approximate date he would need to return for service as mares generally come "in season" about eight days after foaling. A follow-up or two might be necessary to ensure that a new baby colt would be born in the spring.

It was of utmost importance for our cow to calve once a year, because without freshening, she would go dry and there wouldn't be any milk for the table. Each year, shortly after the birth of a new calf, Dad or one of the older brothers would take the cow for a walk. We youngsters couldn't understand why the cow needed to be taken from its baby calf and exercised, as it roamed the hills all day long—until we became old enough to assume the responsibility of walking the cow. A local farmer with several milk cows generally owned a bull, and nearby families with just a family cow or two bargained for breeding services. By keeping a careful watch on the cow's daily deportment following the birth of the last calf, and relying on the calendar, a family member would know the approximate date to lead the cow to the neighboring farm for service. This would be educated guesswork, and sometimes the trip would need to be repeated in a day or so as the biological time clock of the cow did not always coincide with the days of the calendar.

My first walk with the cow is well-remembered. Leading her with a halter rope, we meandered through the woods on the eastern path to Bear Creek and turned east on an old haul road that led toward the neighbor's farm, before entering the pasture field where his cattle were grazing. This route was much safer than trying to lead the cow along the highway where traffic might spook her. As we entered the barn lot, a fenced area used as a staging lot for the milk cows, a loud bellowing sound from inside the barn broke the tranquillity of the early summer morning, followed by the charge of a giant long-horned bull in our direction. As the sound of the rushing hoof beats became more ominous, it was realized that this was not the time for a young lad to be in the midst of this confrontation. After dropping the halter rope and scurrying over the barnyard fence—and anxious to observe the commotion in the barn lot—it was easy to ascertain the object of the affection of the barnyard bull. After a couple of hours, the farmer advised that it was safe to lead the reluctant cow from the barnyard. The old bull didn't offer any resistance, as he was now lying in the shade of an apple tree, docile and chewing his cud, as we exited the barnyard gate on our way home. Early spring, the cow freshened, and the family had milk on the table for another year.

The Depression years ushered in great hardship to both rural and urban families throughout America. To alleviate the suffering of so many who were living in poverty, the federal government instituted a relief program and began to buy meat and vegetable produce from farmers to distribute to the unemployed who were in a dire situation of economic decline. These offerings provided some of the most essential necessities for the table, such as beans, rice, peanut butter, oleo margarine with coloring on the side, fruits, and vegetables. One of the fruits offered was grapefruit, not a favorite, most likely because we were unfamiliar with its preparation for the table, but nothing was ever thrown away! We called it the relief program, and felt somewhat like a popular Midwestern comic who joked that his folks were too poor to paint and too proud to whitewash! In our home we had no aspirations of doing either.

Most families hated to ask for relief, and those who participated in the welfare program early on was the butt of many jokes, but necessity compelled many of our families to set aside all pride and join the program. These offerings became a weekly blessing, and millions of families suffering unemployment were greatly assisted by these necessary staples. Some families were in such dire need that they would send members to the distribution station to wait until the end of the day to pick up any offerings that may have gone unclaimed. Our neighbors to the north trudged past our house, taking this shortcut to Bear Creek, to get their weekly distributions as we did. Though we werc all in the same boat, so to speak, some of the older boys acted less than gentlemanly toward them as they composed and sang uncomplimentary songs to express their contempt as a family member trudged by with a sack of relief stuff.

Another program instituted by the federal and state governments during the Depression years was referred to as old age pension. Many families who owned their homes were as poor as everyone else because there was very little currency to buy the necessities of life. The government followed certain guidelines when issuing old age pension stipends. One guideline stated that a person who owned a designated amount of land or property was deemed to be ineligible for assistance. This rule required the elderly to deed their farms and homes to one of their children to qualify for benefits. Grandma McElhaney deeded the homestead to Dad, and subsequently became eligible to draw a monthly stipend, amounting to ten or fifteen dollars each month. When Grandma began drawing her monthly check, she enjoyed a few of the amenities that made life more bearable, and some of us were a little bit envious of her newfound wealth. She was living a better life than she had enjoyed for many years, even though she no longer owned the country farm.

There were some pitfalls to be considered when parents deeded their land to one of their children. It was rumored that the parents of our aunt's husband, who owned considerable acreage, transferred the title of their farm to their son and began to enjoy the income from the old age pension program. Unfortunately, their plan did not turn out to be foolproof, because in this occurrence, their son became ill and died while his parents were still living. He had previously been engaged in matrimony, which for some reason ended, and he returned home to live with his parents. However, a son who had been born to the couple became the sole heir to the estate. Lucky boy!

Wood was the main fuel supply, and there was an abundant amount in the woods for both cooking and stoking the fireplace...er, tin stove. We basically used two types of wood for fuel. A wood that burned quickly and produced abundant heat was ideal for the kitchen stove. In the 1930s, a blight killed the chestnut trees on our land, and in just a short time, they began to shed their bark. As the pulp lost its moisture, the trunk changed to a pale/whitish color, making these trees easily spotted in the woods.

After cutting a dead tree and snaking it to the wood yard with the ole horse, two of us boys would wrestle with an old crosscut saw, one pulling and the other pushing, in an attempt to cut enough firewood for cooking. but we finally cut the trunk into sections, each about twelve inches long, and threw them in a pile. These chunks of wood were then split into pieces small enough to be placed into the burner of the stove.

The pulp of the dead chestnut tree was easy to cut with our primitive tools, and one could use an axe to slice thin shavings called kindling from the trunk and use them to start a fire quite easily. Chestnut trees were in limited supply but they were a good source of cooking fuel while they lasted.

The second type of wood was used for heating the house. It would be desirable if the pulp was more dense and a little green, like that of live hickory and oak trees, which would burn longer and keep the fire going throughout the day without having to stoke the stove too frequently. Just before turning in at night, we would plan to have a large oak or hickory chuck of wood, preferably one with a big knot, to place in the burner as it would smolder all night and from that base of live coals, a roaring fire could be built in just a few minutes and warm the house on a cold winter morning. Wood fires leave a residue, or ashes, and they had to be cleaned from the stove daily and spread in the garden. We really derived a benefit from these ashes, as they contained a chemical called potash, an important mineral found in fertilizer.

The wood yard inspired about as much contention between us siblings as any other spot on the farm, as it required almost as much effort to provide fuel for household needs as it did to put food on the table. Of necessity, we children learned to wield the axe and crosscut saw at a very early age, though both of these tools were very dangerous, especially when youngsters were easily provoked when using them. Tempers often flared as we accused each other for not pulling his own weight, and undesirable comments often permeated the atmosphere of the ole wood yard before enough fuel was carried into the house to cook our meals and keep us warm throughout the night, but come evening, there was generally an ample supply by the stove to keep the house warm. In retrospect, very few of us fancied that phase of our lives.

We were all exposed to harrowing experiences with these tools when chopping wood, as the ax might come off the handle on a down swing, causing potential harm to anyone close by. When the axe was swung on an angle in an attempt to remove chips from a log, it might strike the log awkwardly and cause the one who was using it to lose control, with potential harm to himself or anyone else in the nearby vicinity. Most wood yards had a chopping block, a large tree trunk which was cut about twelve inches long, and when it was placed on one end, it made a solid foundation for chopping wood or shaving kindling. This also caused one to work well above the ground level and presented a hazard, as the ax might glance when shaving kindling and present a danger to one's lower extremities.

Our individual wardrobe was a continuous problem, as the family had very limited resources. It was necessary to make as many clothes for the family as possible, and most of the materials that were readily available were empty feed sacks. In most cases, both outer and inner garments were made from this material. As one can imagine, the female members of the family had a more difficult time with their wardrobe than did us boys, who seldom if ever wore undergarments.

When an older child grew out of an article of clothing, it would be handed down to a smaller member who could wear it. When new clothes were purchased for the family, they were generally for older family members, and the younger ones often got leftovers, or hand-me-downs. We younger ones were told how nice those hand-me-downs were because many of the articles that were passed down were decorated with numerous multicolored patches that had been sown on the garment to extend its life.

The same procedure occurred with shoes. Someone in the family was always in need of a pair of shoes when there were none to pass on. In due time, when funds became available, Dad would cut a stick and measure the length of our feet. The next time he went to town, he selected a pair of shoes in which the stick could be inserted, and some fortunate member would be wearing a brand-new pair of one-dollar shoes the next day. If the shoes happened to be a little too tight or too short, we had to make a choice, wear tight shoes or go barefooted, as it might be a long time before they could be returned to the store and exchanged for another pair. If we kept them, they would soon be passed on down to the next younger one in the family.

If the soles of our shoes wore out before the uppers, they would be replaced with stick-on rubber soles, which could be purchased at the local grocery store. The soles were fastened at the toe of the shoe with brads, and trimmed along the sides to fit the existing sole of the shoe. When the heels of our shoes became worn out and needed to be replaced, Dad got out the iron last, an iron block molded to fit in inside of a shoe, to make the necessary repairs. When the last was fastened onto a solid foundation, it provided a solid base to clinch the brads and secure the heels to the shoes. If the brads didn't clinch properly, sharp ends of the brads would protrude through the inner sole and dig into our feet, and we would be going barefooted until repairs could be made. However, going barefooted wasn't a burden, unless it was in very cold weather, as we all went barefooted during warm weather.

During the winter snows, we seldom wore overshoes or rubber boots to protect out feet and legs, but when the snow was quite deep, we wrapped our legs below the knees with feed sacks and secured them with twine string to protect our lower extremities from the elements of nature.

4. Family Responsibilities

Each family member, beginning at a very early age, was expected to contribute with the daily chores, and during the summer, work in the fields. We were all in action very early in the day to milk the cow(s) and feed the domestic animals, generally a horse or mule, a cow, a few chickens, and a pig or two. While some were working in the wood yard, the barn or chicken house, others were in the kitchen preparing the meal of the day. During the year when school was in session, activity around our home began well before daybreak, as all the chores had to be completed and breakfast prepared for several hungry siblings. With one outhouse and one wash pan to wash our faces, very little time was wasted as we scurried about in our preparation to catch the school bus at eight each morning, a mile down the hill.

The older members of the family walked through the woods on the most eastern path that led to the Bear Creek area and attended a one-room school that was located on lower Bear Creek during the twenties and early thirties. It was about a two-mile walk each way, and with the school day consuming most of the daylight hours, and having chores before and after school, these days were long indeed! Arriving home at five in the evening, everyone scrambled to finish the chores as darkness began to settle over the land and bring another day to an end. (The coal oil lantern was an important source of illumination since our morning chores were often completed before daylight and the evenings chores well after dark, especially during the winter months.)

Work on the farm was somewhat mundane throughout the year, and all activities were predictable. We were forever cutting wood and carrying it into the house for heating and cooking. An adequate supply of water had to be drawn for the next morning's use before our work was finished. Cooking was the most demanding of all chores for us youngsters, and Dad was not a person who exhibited much expertise in the kitchen, simply because he didn't have time and it wasn't customary for men to cook in that age. After our mother and older sister passed away in the late thirties, the responsibility for the preparation of our meals fell on the shoulders of the oldest sibling at home. Since few of us children knew very much about this important necessity, cooking really became a hardship for us.

Most meals were usually very bland, often consisting of beans and potatoes and some kind of bread. The quantity and quality of our cooking left a lot to be desired, and the phrase "burnt beans" was frequently heard at our kitchen table, but complaining worked both ways as the time came when each of us had to take a turn at the cookstove! Finally, our younger sister assumed responsibility for the cooking chores. She did a good job, and we remaining boys at home were happy to be relieved from the cooking business.

The quantity of a food item to be cooked would be determined by the size of the jar in which it was stored, such as a half gallon jar of green beans or tomatoes. We were fortunate if we had more than one serving of bread each meal, as we had just one baking pan and baking bread was time-consuming, making it almost impossible to bake twice for the same meal.

The tableware at each place setting consisted of a tin plate, sometimes a tin cup, and a spoon. Cooking utensils served double duty. After being used for cooking the fare for that meal, they were set on the table and used as serving dishes. Following the meal, the table utensils had to be washed, which habitually provoked an interlude of bickering, but in finality, the pots and pans would be passed through the dishpan water, dried, and hung on nails or stored in the cupboard. Three meal preparations each day were certainly more drudgery than pleasure!

When Grandad McElhaney died in 1929, our family became the surrogate caretaker for Grandma, who was nearly seventy years of age and living alone. This simply meant that we cared for two households instead of one. Two supplies of wood, two gardens to weed and hoe, water for two households to be drawn and carried, running to the grocery store for staples, and sometime during our childhood, each of us took our turn staying at night with Grandma.

Staying all night with Grandma, especially during the summer months, meant that we were to be at her house at least by sunset or earlier each evening, as Grandma always retired near twilight time. If the assigned one didn't darken her front door by sundown, her cry from the rear door of her house could be heard throughout our little valley, and the delinquent party's tardiness came to an abrupt end.

Before bedtime, Grandma always read the Bible and said her prayers, sometimes to the displeasure of her captive audience. One can still remember old Pharaoh getting trapped in the Red Sea and all of his soldiers drowning. Elijah called fire down from heaven several times each week to defeat Israel's enemies. It seemed as though Jonah was swallowed by the whale every three or four days. Very few of us boys relished this assignment, especially during summertime, as we had to go to bed while the others were still at play, but our little sister has remarked that staying with Grandma was a very special time in her life when we were living on the hill. She loved Grandma's stories, and those moments were very important to her in her young years.

During the winter months, the nights were very long for the one to be at Grandma's house soon after the evening chores were finished. The next morning, the one who stayed with Grandma crawled out of bed well before daylight, dressed in the cold, and went home to do the chores, and after breakfast, it was off to school. This arrangement was a daily requirement for some lucky grandchild until Grandma fell and broke her hip in the late forties. Following this accident, she was forced to leave the hill for the first time in well over a decade, and live with her daughter on Camp Creek until her death. When it was determined that she would not return to her home, Dad and the three remaining children at home moved into her house, which was but a change in residence with little or no enhancement in living conditions.

Generally, the oldest sibling at home was responsible for a smooth routine of the day while Dad was at work on the WPA. When Mom died, there were six of us children at home whose ages ranged between four and fifteen, and we were expected to carry on with the household and farming duties under the supervision of the oldest member at home. Occasionally, a younger member of the clan might rebel against the authority of the one in charge. If the younger one could run fast enough to escape, the woods offered refuge until Dad returned home that evening, and hopefully the conundrum would be taken into advisement with relief, but tomorrow was another day, and we learned to live the best we could. While sibling leadership was not the best form of family government, it was all we had. We grew up quickly!

We each took our turn at cleaning house, but this was generally the responsibility of the older members, as many household duties required a more mature person. In summer, it seemed as if Monday morning came twice each week, as that was the day to do the laundry, and all who weren't in the fields or doing other domestic duties were engaged in the laundry activity! Saturday was wash day during the months we attended school.

The care of the livestock was time-consuming—all year long. Each spring, we used the currying brush and removed the winter hair from the horses. The horses would stand still for grooming, but for some reason, we didn't dare to tackle the cows. The old barn needed to be cleaned periodically. We pitched the manure to the outside through two small windows at the rear of the stalls before spreading a layer of corn stalks in the stalls for bedding. Come spring, the manure at the rear of the barn had to be removed, as those manure piles had grown to large mounds of garden fertilizer. Those of us who engaged in the cleanup knew we were in for several days' work as we hooked up the team and began loading the manure onto the sled with a pitchfork. When loaded, the sled was then dragged to the gardens and the manure was scattered over the ground in preparation for spring plowing.

Like other children of our age, we tried to find ways to escape some of our chores, but when an extra hand was really needed for a job, it wasn't hard to find someone who was shirking his duty, as we all had developed certain patterns in our lifestyle. When the fruit was beginning to ripen, one particular sibling could likely be found in the cherry, apple, or peach tree, or wandering through the berry patches. Another liked to get away by himself to explore the fields and woods. Of course, we all used the excuse of having a headache or bellyache from time to time—often truthfully—when the job to be performed was boring. Most of the time, our duties were so repetitious or aggravating that we might just walk off the job, if we were old enough to get by with it. Through the years, though, we did learn the importance of responsibility and before we left the hill, each of us more than pulled his own weight when doing the farm chores and taking care of the home.

5. Struggle for Survival

Dad had never held a job that afforded a regular income during the decade of the twenties, excepting a short duration at the N&W Railroad freight house in Portsmouth. Living nearly twenty miles from the center of employment and not owing an automobile made it reasonably impracticable to continue working for the railroad. Most employment was short-lived anyway, as the commerce of the nation was grinding to a snail's pace with the advent of the Great Depression in the early thirties. Therefore, our livelihood was dependent on the resources of the land and what little produce we could glean from the farm.

One could say at best that our farming methods were

very crude, and our enterprise could most certainly be referred to as "hard-scrabble" farming. It was not very rewarding to work all spring and summer in the fields to plant, till, care for a couple acres of hay and corn, and reap a harvest that barely provided enough feed to winter the few animals we owned until the grass began to grow the next spring. Lime and fertilizer were hardly an option for farmers of that day, and the only supplement available to enrich the soil was plain ole barnyard manure, which in our situation was desperately needed for the two gardens. Without using fertilizer or practicing crop rotation to replenish the nutrients in the soil, the crop yield declined year by year.

We farmed the same fields each year until the ground wore out. When that was determined, a distress call would go out for more new land. When the old land was used up, it was laid to rest, and would subsequently grow over with brush. Years later, after it had rested, and believing the soil had regenerated, we would grub the brush and make plans to put the field back into production. This brought about considerable whining and groaning from all of us children who, upon reaching the stature of being physically strong enough to wield an axe and grubbing hoe, knew that the next few weeks would not be pleasant ones.

Grubbing was using these unwieldy tools to clear the land of brush, roots, and stumps. The brush and small saplings would be cut and piled to dry and burned at a later time. A mattock was used to clear the soil from the roots so that they could be chopped from the stump. Following that procedure, we would hook a chain around the stump and attempt to pull it from the ground with the horse. Imagine that it may take a half hour or so to pull one stump, and looking around you would see an acre or so of them to be removed! How many plots of new land we reclaimed or how much virgin land we cleared and put into farm production during those years, no one really knows.

Grubbing wasn't finished when the field was plowed and the crops planted. Parts of the underground roots remained intact regardless of how careful we were in trying to remove them, and being alive, they sprouted and grew throughout the growing season, requiring further removal of the foliage to allow the crops to receive all available nourishment from the ground. Likewise, before planting the next year, another grubbing session was required to remove any roots that may have surfaced because the ground was constantly freezing and thawing throughout the winter months.

Having removed the stumps and roots, the next process would be preparing the ground for planting. Harrowing experiences might come upon one when plowing new ground. A long pair of leather reins that was used to control the horses was an important part of the harness. These reins were tied or buckled together at the ends, and when plowing, they were adjusted to a desired length and placed above one shoulder and under the other by the person that was plowing. This arrangement gave control over the horse while it freed our hands to wrestle with the plow, which was no easy feat in that rough ground.

A person plowing in this manner would become harnessed in between the handles of the plow in front and the leather reins around the shoulders, which, of course, were attached to the bridle of a thousand-pound horse! If a whiffletree (single-tree or double-tree)—a wooden crossbar with metal hooks on each end to attach the harness chains—broke, or the point of the plow struck a big root that was missed during the grubbing procedure—not a rare occurrence—one would likely be jerked hard against the crossbar that supported the plow handles and would be quite fortunate to escape from getting bruised or severely injured!

When plowing new ground, there would be many hidden roots and it was difficult to do much more than just scratch the surface. It was almost impossible for the plow to dig in six or seven inches until the ground had been plowed a few times. Shovel plows, when used in the preparation of new ground, would do the job just as well as the breaking plow, as the top soil was generally soft and easy to penetrate.

If the field in production was situated on a hillside, a hillside breaking plow worked well. The plow section of the hillside plow swivelled at the point where it fastened to the beam. At the end of the field, the plow was swung one hundred eighty degrees, reversing the direction the soil would be turned and allowing the land to be plowed by going back and forth, always turning the soil in the direction below the plow.

Farm land was generally depleted of minerals from raising crops year after year without the benefit of fertilizers and legumes. In the early forties, the government inaugurated programs to help farmers in various areas of soil conservation and land management. Several local farmers submitted applications to the soil enrichment program for assistance. Our request was approved, and a truck load of lime was dumped along the road at the mouth of the hollow, a mile away. It became our responsibility to haul, drag, or carry that lime to the farm over an uphill craggy road with inadequate horse power and equipment, and spread it on the ground by hand.

It didn't take too many loads to cause damage to the wagon wheels, leaving only a sled to drag the lime up to the farm. This project turned into a long summer job because we could just move a small jag of heavy lime on a sled with a team of crippled animals. If we hauled a couple loads each day, we had managed a good day's work. The "law of diminishing returns" applied to this project, as many hours of labor were invested without a noticeable increase in production.

Our main field crops were corn, oats, and hay. These species were selected as the sole purpose of farming was to provide feed for the chickens, a hog or two, a cow, and sometimes a team of horses. In many ways, corn was the most difficult and time-consuming crop to raise. After plowing, we would drag and harrow the ground until it was worked well enough to cover the seeds so they would germinate. After the soil had been prepared for planting, we hitched the horse to a shovel plow and made furrows through the field, about three feet apart. The seed would then be dropped into the furrow, by hand, and one of us kids followed with a hoe and covered the seed with about two inches of topsoil.

Farmers believed that corn needed to be plowed at least three or four times to grow a good crop, and after the corn had sprouted and grown a few inches tall, it was time to do more plowing. The corn plow consisted of a straight horizontal beam made of steel or wood. Two or more branches were attached to the beam about a foot apart and curved downward toward the ground. A colter, or shovel, was bolted to the foot of each branch, with one colter trailing the other and slightly offset to the rear. When plowing, we attempted to get close to the corn row to dig out as many weeds as possible without rooting the small plants from the ground. Yet one more pass between the rows, and the bulk, needed to be made to control all of the weeds. This method required three passes for each row of corn, and at that rate, an acre of corn meant a lot of plowing!

Corn was harvested the old-fashioned way. It was cut and shocked in late summer, about September, while the leaves were still green, but after the ears had matured. The shock pattern was laid out to position the shocks about thirty feet apart. We then tied the tops of four corn stocks together, forming a bridgework resembling a teepee. We would start working on a single row, cutting each stock close to the ground with a long corn knife. One would have an armload by the time he reached the next shock. This was a laborious job, as every stock of corn in the field would be cut and carried to the shocks.

It was generally hot in the cornfield, with few breezes to give the workers relief. To protect ourselves from cuts and scratches from the sharp edges of the leaves of the corn, it was important to wear a long-sleeved shirt to protect our arms. In addition, a soft cloth wrapped around our neck was necessary to protect that part of our body. These conditions resulted in a hot job, and cutting and shocking a small field of corn was no small task for youngsters, especially when the corn was much taller than we were.

The corn, being somewhat green, remained in the shocks to dry, or ripen, and late in the fall it would be husked and stored in the corn crib. The fodder—dried corn stalks—was stacked in the barn to feed the animals during the winter. After they had eaten the dried leaves and chewed the stalks for any nourishing substance, the remains were subsequently used as barn bedding. Thus, all parts of the crop were used in one manner or another. We were fortunate to raise an ample supply of feed for the chickens, cows, pigs, and horses; therefore, selling any portion of the crop for cash was out of the question.

The lowland farmers, whose acreage lay adjacent to the Scioto River, hired neighboring farmers for the harvest season who owned a team and wagon and were willing to work in the fields to harvest the corn. When the harvest season set in, one would see four or five outfits in the field at one time. If one husker could husk and crib two loads of corn a day—each load containing about thirty bushels—he would have done a good day's work, and would have earned about five or six dollars for that day's work. The corn was husked from standing stocks and occasionally the horses, in an attempt to snitch an ear of corn to eat, knocked some of it on the ground.

To supplement lean seasons of production at home, we would drive our horse and wagon to the bottoms and glean corn from the fields that had been harvested. Scouring a large corn field might produce a couple bushels of corn in an afternoon, which was enough to feed our animals for several days.

If possible, we planned to have a patch of oats and two species of hay for winter feed. Horses like timothy hay, a tall grass-like plant that produces a large quantity of feed on a small plot of ground. It was believed that clover hay was the best feed for the production of milk, and for the bovines we raised Lespedeza, a species of the clover family.

Following the general preparation of the soil, oats and hay, being grass-like crops, were sown with a hand seeder, a method we referred to as broadcasting. After sowing, a harrow was dragged over the field to cover the seed, and if these crops sprouted and grew, we would be finished with them until time for harvest, sometime in early or mid-July. Both crops were harvested by using the same method. Early on, a scythe was the only implement suitable for cutting a grass crop, but using this strange implement for a few hours was akin to doing hard labor on a rock pile. No one looked forward to a day in the hayfield with a scythe in hand! Later on, we somehow acquired an old McCormick Deering mowing machine to mow crops of this nature.

After the hay crops were mowed, they were left on the ground for about three days to cure, or dry, depending on weather conditions. Following this curing period, the hay was raked into doodles with pitchforks and loaded on a sled or wagon and hauled to the barn.

We later constructed a rake that was pulled by the horse. It consisted of twenty-five or thirty narrow boards, or slats, about two feet long, two or three inches in width, sharpened on one end and nailed to a long header board or pole about three inches apart. Footers, large wooden stakes that slid along the ground at the rear, held the rake at a desirable angle for raking glass-like crops. Long handles were extended to the rear for control and dumping. With the horse tethered at the front with several feet of rope, we raked perpendicular to the mowing swath and scooped up the hay until the rake was full. The rake would be dumped by flipping the handles forward, releasing the hay when it was turned upside down. With a little practice, one could lay out a fairly straight windrow that made it easier to stack the hay in doodles, the last task to be executed before hauling the hay to the barn. Seldom did we manage to finish raking hay in the field before one or more of the slats struck a rock or a hard place in the ground, requiring down time for another repair job, but this method was much quicker and easier than raking and stacking the hay with a pitchfork.

Tall tales were common concerning the trials when working with domesticated animals. When we were working in the fields, seldom did any of us have a pocket watch, and we would judge when it was time to stop for dinner by the way our stomach felt and how high the sun was in the sky (if it wasn't cloudy), but mostly the sound of a freight train whistle was a signal for quitting the job for dinner.

The main north/south lines of the N&W Railroad were laid out along the eastern side of the Scioto River. These trains, powered by giant steam engines that hauled thousands of tons of coal from the coal fields in the Appalachian Mountain area to industrial centers in the north, required a considerable amount of water for their boilers. A large water tower, located across the Scioto River from our hill farm, became a main stop to fill the boilers of those thirsty engines. It just happened that about eleven thirty each weekday morning, a train pulled into the watering station with its shrilling whistle emitting a musical crescendo that permeated the hills and valleys for miles around. To us children who were working in the fields, that whistle was like the sound of sweet music, announcing the dinner hour and a period of welcomed rest. But not to us kids alone!

At one time, we owned a small black mule that became accustomed to returning to the barn at the sound of the train whistle so that it became a hassle to continue to work him in the field any longer. He was just as hungry and tired, or contrary, as we were. One particular day we quit a few minutes early and arrived at the gate below our house just as the train whistle alarmed the countryside that it was quitting time. That darn mule began to chomp at the bit to get to the barn and crowded the gate so close that we had to really jerk the reins to keep him under control. If he could have talked, he would likely have told us that his momma didn't raise any dummies and it was time to eat!

Living in a backwoods country, we worked the land and took whatever it had to offer. We lived from the fruits of the land and needed little income except for a few staples that made life more bearable. We had no such expenses as insurance, income taxes or licenses, but a state sales tax was imposed at the rate of about 1 percent on purchases other than food, which didn't affect us very much. All landowners were required to pay a small levy for property tax, and for us that became a burden once every year, although it was a meager amount. In some instances, the homeowner was allowed to work on public roads to pay his property tax bill. There were other needs and occasional emergencies, however, that did require a little money. These occasions required us to use other amenities of the farm to raise emergency funds.

Our farm contained a large variety of deciduous trees that could be sold for cash if there was a market for wood products. Locust posts, after being cut and debarked, were sold for a few cents each. Cotton wood was another source of income. Poplar, or any wood distinguished by soft pulp, would be cut in eight-foot lengths—we used an eight-foot pole to measure the cut—and hauled to the river road to sell to a trucker who in turn sold the wood to the paper mill. This cotton wood was used to manufacture paper and cardboard products. The demand for paper products rose sharply after the war started, providing a needed source of income for our family. During the summer months when the ground was dry, and if the road was passable, a trucker might drive up the hill to pick up a load of pulp wood, which saved us the many trips that were needed to haul that much pulp wood to the highway. Any such attempt by a trucker to haul timber from the hill when the ground was soft practically destroyed the roadbed, as chains installed on the drive wheels of the truck tended to cut deep ruts in the road, requiring several hours of work to repair the damage!

Large trunks of hardwood trees, called cross ties, were used to lay the foundation for railroad tracks, and when a market existed for cross ties, we would go into the woods and hew out a load which provided a little money for household needs. Producing a cross tie by hand was a laborious process that required selecting and felling a proper-sized oak tree, dragging it out of the woods with a horse, cutting the trunks to the required length of eight feet, and preparing it for sale.

We began producing a cross tie by scoring two sides of the log at close intervals with a timber axe. A broad axe, a short-handled axe with a wide blade that was slightly offset, was used to remove or hew the scoured area from the log, and when finished, two sides of the trunk resembled a flat plane. It was required that we maintain the thickness of the trunk to be eight inches throughout its length. After debarking the other two sides, which were left in a round shape, one would have a finished cross tie to meet the standards of the railroad. After the cross ties were finished, we hauled them to the river road, which was somewhat more than a mile, and sold them to a trucker for about a dollar each. Once in a while, in earlier years and if the farm wagon was in good repair, we hauled the ties to the railroad station ourselves and didn't have to pay the middle man.

Frequently, Dad took us boys to the woods when he was making ties or cutting posts. We learned early on in life the meaning of work, and we helped in felling and trimming the trees and clearing the site so that the trunk could be cut into manageable proportions that could be removed from the woods. Felling timber and using sharp instruments like the axe and crosscut saw were dangerous work and we were very fortunate to escape without harming ourselves to any degree.

Occasionally, we boys picked berries to sell to a family on Bear Creek. One summer, a couple of us boys picked a gallon of blackberries and delivered them as requested, for which we received one-half dollar. The family patriarch, whom we later referred to as an old curmudgeon, desired a gallon of huckleberries, and agreed to pay us a dollar a gallon upon delivery. Picking a gallon of huckleberries was no small task, but we promptly filled and delivered the order and contracted for another gallon to be delivered the next week. We delivered the berries as promised, but he welshed on the deal and would only pay us seventy-five cents. We were naturally disappointed, but being young boys, we didn't have the expertise to bargain for the extra advantage. It wasn't so much about the lesser amount of money we received; it was the principle involved as he bragged that since we settled for the amount he paid us, he would never again pay us the original bargained price—and we never picked berries for him again. Even in hard times, we felt we had to take a stand on principles, even if it was costly for us.

In the thirties, a large percentage of American workers were without jobs and became eligible to enroll in various public work programs designed to alleviate unemployment and to recharge the economy during the Depression years. Conservation camps were operated throughout the country to build public parks and recreational facilities, but the real purpose was to provide jobs for young single men. Those who participated lived at the working site in what was referred to as CCC camps. The WPA was a program for unemployed family men. Those jobs were generally close to home, and for the most part the men worked on public institutions, such as roads, water works, dams, school buildings, and county and city municipal buildings.

Dad was employed during the later years of the thirties by the sector that was in charge of building roads. He would rise early and was off to work before we kids were out of bed, as he frequently had to walk to the job. Travel to and from work was a long and laborious task, leaving little time for him to be with the family and engage in domestic responsibilities. Most of the public road building works were executed by hand labor, using crude tools. The laborers' hours were spent by digging and shoveling dirt from the edges of the road—referred to as ditching—which provided drainage and prevented erosion of the road surface. The excess dirt was moved by wheelbarrow and used in areas where the road needed to be repaired.

By the early forties, with the wind of war looming over the nation, industrial jobs were becoming more available, causing most public work programs to be eliminated, a decision that was soon to leave Dad and many others like him without jobs. Our livelihood now depended on farming and selling the resources of the land.

While on summer recess from school, those of us who were old enough attempted to find work from the local farmers. Most farm work was performed by hand labor during this period, and labor was cheap, which made it a little easier for teenage boys to find part-time jobs. However, some local farmers would take advantage of young boys and work them in the fields for substandard wages. Making hay on a hot afternoon and receiving a quarter for the service would help one remember that life was not always peaches and cream, neither was it fair! When we were hired for a full day's work, we were expected to work from seven in the morning until six in the evening, with an hour off for lunch.

Bottom land that lay along the Scioto River was considered the best farmland because it flooded quite often. The flood waters carried enriched soil from land upstream and deposited it on acreage situated along the river. The downside of these floods was the saturation of the land with unwanted seeds that produced an abundance of undesirable weeds. Two species of these weeds, the horse weed and Johnson grass, were the most numerous and both were very difficult to control. They grew much faster than the corn and it wasn't an unusual sight to see eight or ten workers, summer help, cutting weeds with a hoe in a hundred-acre cornfield with a couple adults working alongside and supervising the inexperienced help. Johnson grass was especially difficult to chop out of the corn rows, and by the time we had chopped it from a row of corn, our hoes were in need of being sharpened...and we needed a break period. We enjoyed the camaraderie of working together, and though we relished the break at the end of the field, we were noted for pulling pranks on each other while resting and sharpening our hoes in preparation to hack out the next row.

One instance that this writer is reminded of to this day was bragging how sharp he had filed his hoe and how easily those weeds would fall as we worked our way toward the other end of the field. A buddy who was anxious to verify the words of this braggart grabbed the hoe handle to inspect the blade. That action resulted in the end of work for that day and a trip to the local doctor as the sharp blade of the hoe came in contact with his right thumb. The hoe was the winner and that scar is a timely reminder sixty years later that boys will be boys.

We observed an hour for lunch each day, and a large sycamore tree near the entrance of the corn crib afforded a cool and pleasant place to rest before the afternoon session began. Most youngsters regenerate quickly, and before returning to work, it was rare that some of us didn't engage in a little mischief. The nearby corn crib provided a good source of ammunition and we sometimes challenged each other to do battle in a corn cob fight. One must stake out a safe haven if he didn't want to return to work with welts on his person. A good place to hide for protection was the granary, but if one was cornered and charged from both ends, it was very difficult to surmount a defense. A few well-placed strikes on the head and arms kept our body parts smarting most of the afternoon.

The leader of our crew was a middle-aged man who enjoyed country music and had a little talent in singing and imitating the country stars. His presence made the day go better as he entertained us both in the field while we were working and at lunchtime. Probably his best imitation was that of the trains visiting the water station located just across the river. He would use the wood floor in the corn crib as a stage, and by shuffling his boots on the wooden floor to the imaginary movements of the steam engines while vocalizing their sounds, he could vividly portray the train slowing to a stop, imitate the gurgling sounds that could be heard when the trains were taking on water for their boilers, and shuffle his feet to imitate the laborious act of the engines as they were starting the long trains again. Sometimes, his antics made the noon hour pass too quickly, and we were soon back in the fields working.

Harvesting wheat was a hot job, but it was a memorable event that involved many of the community farmers who raised that crop. Near the beginning of July after the wheat had matured, farmers cut their wheat with a binder that also tied it into sheaves, or small bundles. The sheaves were shocked by hand and left in the field to cure, or ripen. About mid-July, there would be a "threshing festival" in that community. Farmers who owned a threshing machine made a circuit throughout the various communities to thresh the local farmers' wheat. The owner of the threshing machine, which was powered by a giant steam engine, set up his equipment at a predetermined location to oblige the surrounding farmers who desired his services. Local farmers were responsible for hiring help to keep the threshing machine busy.

Having the wheat cut, sheaved, shocked, and cured, a large threshing gang would begin hauling it to the thresher with horses and wagons. It wasn't unusual to see a half dozen farmers with their teams and wagons hauling wheat to the threshing station from the surrounding farms. Two people working on the ground tossed the sheaves to the person who was loading the wagon. When a wagon was loaded, it was pulled alongside the thresher and the sheaves were thrown on the conveyer with a pitchfork, heads first. The teamster had to be careful not to drive his horses too close to the belt and pulley on the threshing machine, as the horses constantly switched their tails in fighting flies and could get their tails caught in the pulley mechanism, causing severe injury. After the threshing machine separated the wheat from its stock, it would be dispensed through a shoot to one side of the thresher and collected in large grain sacks. The straw was blown to the straw stack located on the other side of the threshing machine.

Threshing day was an unforgettable time for all, including housewives and other farm family members. The women enjoyed threshing day as well as anyone. They planned and cooked the threshing dinners, and the quality of the abundant food was never lacking. After gorging ourselves with roast beef, ham, country fried chicken, and the supporting amenities that made a complete threshing meal, washed down with glasses of iced tea and topped off with fresh apple or blackberry pie, we desired to lie in the shade for a spell to allow our dinners to settle. But most of the work lay ahead and it would be a long afternoon before the fields were bare and the wheat had been stored in the granary.

After the threshing machine had moved to another

community, all that remained to be done was baling the straw with a stationary baler, generally powered with a small air-cooled engine. The baler was stationed near the straw stack and the straw was pitched onto the baler conveyer by hand. The bales were stacked nearby until each farmer claimed his share. Each participating farmer was obliged to account for his share and haul his straw home.

There was an apple orchard about four miles west on the Bear Creek road, and when the apples had ripened, some of us boys would get up early and walk—a distance of about four miles—to the Sedan area to pick apples. Ten cents and hours in the fields or ten cents a bushel for picking apples was the going rate for both farmers and orchard keepers, but we were contented to get what little work that was available. After climbing those apple trees all day long and struggling with an apron loaded with apples, we were happy to see the evening roll around and were tired youngsters by the time we had walked back home, but not much richer.

Our older brothers worked on farms several miles north of us as hired hands and would room and board with the farm family. The northen farmers planted large acreage of corn, and needed several laborers for the harvest. Many went north during late summer to cut corn, which was subsequently tied into shocks and left in the fields to dry. In middle autumn, they might return to husk and crib the corn and shred the fodder. Several unemployed family men earned extra money in this manner, but they had to leave their families for the duration of the harvest.

Locally, one might find employment at a sawmill. Inexperienced workers were always assigned to the lofty position of tender, or off bearing—that is, after the slabs had been cut from a log in an attempt to square it for lumber, the tender would grab a couple of them and carry them to the slab pile, which might be several yards away. When the mill was down, the tender had the responsibility to remove the sawdust from the mill site. At best, one might make a couple of dollars a day, often having to wait until a load of lumber was sold before receiving his pay.

There were sand and gravel bars along the larger creeks and the township trustees often hired local farmers who owned a team of horses and a gravity wagon to haul gravel and build or repair the county and township roads. The bed of a gravel wagon consisted of strong wooden slats that lay loose on crossing frames. These slats protruded beyond the end boards for about a foot, providing a hand hold for workers on each end of the wagon to flip the slats on their edges, allowing the gravel to fall to the road where it would be spread to repair the road bed. Several laborers would also be hired to shovel the gravel onto the wagons to be hauled to the sight where the road was being repaired. If money was available, local labor was used to repair bridges and other public works, and for the upkeep of the township house and local cemeteries. Most people were appreciative of the supplemental income and desired to work several days a year in the public domain.

Having a few cents in your pocket gave rise to visit the local grocery store. Most early country grocery stores were generally housed in a room located in the front part of the owner's living quarters. A coal oil lamp or two provided light at the front counter, and could be carried to the storage areas to provide light for the grocer when he was filling a request for a customer. A heating stove, located near the counter, was surrounded with several chairs where the men of the community would congregate on a weekend afternoon or winter evening to swap stories and perhaps purchase a few items before heading home.

Spittoons graced either side of the stove and became targets for unofficial spitting contests. It was seldom decided who was the most accurate with their spittle discharge, but the grocer's last chore of the evening before closing the store was cleaning up the mess.

Flour, beans, and other dry goods were stored in wooden barrels and sold by the pound. An old spring scale was used for weighing those loose items. The soda pop case was cooled with large blocks of ice that were delivered by the ice man each week. There were just a few brands of soda pop to choose from and the price was five cents a bottle. An old meat cooler packed with ice contained a few items of pork or beef, but the popular meat was bologna, as it had been cooked and wrapped tightly for preservation, whereas other fresh meat would be exposed to the air and spoil more quickly.

Most country stores of that day had a front porch with loafing benches, and it was common for an assemblage of adult men to be seen spending a few hours of thc day loafing at the store, especially when unemployment was high. As automobiles became more numerous, gasoline pumps were installed near the front of the store. These pumps were constructed in the shape of a cylinder, about eight feet tall. They featured a glass reservoir near the top that held ten gallons of gasoline and it was filled before dispensing gasoline. Two pipes extended from the gas tank located under the ground to the top of the reservoir, one to pump the gasoline into the reservoir, and the other acted as an overflow pipe which insured the reservoir would be filled properly. A metal lever about three feet long fixed to an inside pump and attached to the side of the pump stand was used to fill the reservoir. Gasoline was dispensed by gravity through a hose long enough to reach the gasoline tank on the automobile.

Knowing we had found summer jobs, the local grocer

might allow some of us youngsters to run up a tab until payday, for such amenities as pop, nickel pies (pineapple was a favorite) and Bugler tobacco to roll your own cigarettes. He was often gracious enough to carry us during the winter months when times were lean, to be paid after work became available the next summer. We desired to maintain good relations with him. He no doubt sympathized with our plight by remembering that he had lived an early life somewhat like we were experiencing.

The Depression and lack of jobs pitted neighbor against neighbor in the field of employment. Working a few hours each week could mean the difference between the family going to bed on a full stomach or eating lean. The term spoils system was used to describe the way public employment was controlled. Most all government jobs were political, as Civil Service laws were yet to be enacted to protect workers' rights. The state of Ohio engineered the building of roads, public works, and buildings, and those who were fortunate to have a job in a government enterprise would likely be members or at least show evidence of being sympathetic to the political party in office. When the state elected a new governor in opposition to the party in office, many public workers lost their jobs. This policy was practiced by politicians at the local level as well as the state level. However, few exceptions might be made for families suffering a financial or health crisis, but rarely did one party have sympathy for members of another party as they had made too many promises to their own supporters.

This winner-take-all practice affected the way people voted for candidates who were running for elected offices. On election day morning, candidates and their supporters gathered near the election hall, and throughout the day attempted to persuade voters to vote their officials into office. Most everyone in the community was concerned by the outcome of the vote. If you were presently working in the public sector and your party's candidate lost the election, your job would also be at risk. On the other hand, the opposition winner would attempt to find jobs for those who supported him. Since election day was a holiday in a sense, there were few other public activities scheduled and the precinct surroundings were nearly always crowded with the candidates and their supporters.

Booze, guns, and threats against opposition voters were frequently present and many voters were intimidated to make the right choices. While modern election laws prohibit loitering in or near the voting precincts, the laws of the twenties and thirties failed to recognize the abuses exerted by a few persons who were desirous of controlling the outcome of the elections.

Most all communities sported politicians or dominant figureheads with advocates, whom they showered with various favors to command their loyalty. These partisans, especially when their jobs were at risk, realized they must support the man who favored them. One such person, "Old Jim," a bootlegger, gambler, and a man of worldly vices, was said to have been involved in several gray areas that were considered to be outside the norms of the community. Old Jim was a person having considerable influence with several members in the community, being favorable to some but detestable to others. He desired to be influential with the outcome of elections and prodded voters to vote to his advantage. At one particular election, there was considerable protest between opposing factions desiring to affect the outcome at the ballot box.

It can be said that liquor, guns, and elections don't mix very well when members of opposing factions have so much at stake on the outcome, which was the case in the heat of one local contest. Bragging, arguing, drinking, and gamesmanship were runners-up to an ensuing brawl that broke out between two rowdies of the rival parties, with the son of Old Jim taking the measure of "Billy," who had been urged to engage in a contest for election yard dominance. When Billy was on the verge of losing the fight, he called for help and his nearby friend and comrade, "Young Bull," responded, as he also seemed to be involved in the courtyard melee. Whether Young Bull carried a gun on his person or not, this election brawl ended with Old Jim's son being shot to death.

When Old Jim received word of the incident, everyone knew that this election day would be remembered for many ages. Realizing the predicament he had gotten himself into, Young Bull gathered a sack of provisions, including his gun and ammunition, said his goodbyes to his family, and headed for the hills in upper Camp Creek, Pike County, a vast forested area which offered refuge for an offender who had run afoul of the law or had lost his good graces in the community, hoping all would blow over in due time.

Old Jim, not one to let the perpetrator of such a horrible deed go unchallenged, assembled a bevy of cronies and headed for the hills with the intent of bringing about justice for the revenge of his son's death. While Young Bull was able to foil the hunting party for several days, he could not contain the army that Old Jim had mustered to exact revenge for the death of his son.

Politics wasn't discussed very much around our home, and Dad never revealed his leaning toward either party, but being a farmer, it could be assumed he was sympathetic toward the Republican party. Our uncles were more vocal and would invoke Roosevelt's name quite often, whether favorable or not—it's been a long time ago and they weren't remembered as people who were particularly fond of politicians. Our neighbor to the north must have leaned toward Roosevelt's party as he was employed with the state highway program during the thirties. While it was low paying and a manual labor job, it provided a living wage for that era. Not only was he employed in the government program, he managed to acquire some of the goodies available to people who participated in the relief program.

This neighbor and his wife walked to the grocery store on weekends after payday, as he didn't own a horse or drive an automobile. Some of us boys liked to joke about their travels, as the wife always "hoofed it" several steps ahead of him and we wondered why they wouldn't walk together. One of the goodies he had acquired was a pair of hobnail shoes, assumably army rations, whose soles and heels were studded with nails having large heads to protect the soles from wearing out so quickly. Observing them walking up the road at dusk one evening and seeing the sparks fly from those hobnailed shoes when his feet scuffed against the macadam road caused us to wonder if he was contemplating how he might come out ahead with their next argument—which he likely didn't—or just attempting to set a fire under her feet to keep her going!

During the later thirties and early forties, war was raging in both the European and Asian theaters, causing great concern about the role America might have to play in world politics. Congress had previously eliminated the monetary system that for years had been controlled by the gold standard, a structured form of economics that limited the ratio of currency in circulation to the value of gold that was stored in the country's treasury vaults. Under this new scheme, the U. S. Treasury began to print and circulate larger amounts of currency that better supplied the needs of a growing population. The manufacturing sector began to awaken from a decade of slumbering, and America was finally on the road to economic recovery, greatly enhanced by the threat of a global war. Part of the unemployment problem ended when many of our young people entered the armed forces and began training for the eventful future, and the military services provided a needed income for those who couldn't find work in the private sector. The world began to turn again.

However, this recovery didn't offer relief to many people living in a rural setting, especially those with large families like ours who were tied to the land. To us, time was pretty much standing still, with our economic conditions changing very little. Public programs that had been in force for several years were grinding to a halt, leaving scores of unemployed people. Myriad of the elderly who found it impossible to move to the manufacturing centers were simply cast back into an era of economic depression.

When a member in our family entered the armed forces, provisions were made for Dad to share in the insurance program that was provided for all armed service personnel should a tragedy occur during the war years. While our family was becoming smaller in numbers, our economic status remained in the doldrums throughout those tumultuous times. When tragedy did come upon us, Dad received a small stipend each month that, while not easing the emotional strain of the loss of a loved one, somewhat lessened the family's financial dilemma, and made it possible for us children who remained at home to continue our education.

6. Our Physical Well-Being

Almost every year, one or two of Mom's sisters would come to our home to visit for a couple of days. We children didn't know why they would rouse us from sleep, generally in the middle of the night, and take us to Grandma's house, but the next morning we returned home and learned we had a new baby brother or sister!

Many expectant mothers living in the rural areas didn't have the luxury of prenatal care, and sometimes they gave birth without the assistance of a doctor. When expectant mothers experienced problems at childbirth, especially without a doctor in attendance, the results could end in tragedy. Infant mortality was very high when children were born under those conditions, and in our family, at least six children died in infancy.

There were no vaccinations for communicable diseases, and when one of us came down with a childhood disease, it was likely to run throughout the family. Some diseases of that day required a family to be quarantined in their home, but in our case, we had freedom of the farm since, by its location, we were practically quarantined from society all the time. One afternoon, while a couple of us small children were taking a nap, so it has been told, the neighbor lady to the north came visiting, a rarity between our families. Her daughter was suffering with the chicken pox, a disease we didn't need, and our family was exposed to another childhood disorder. We really never cared much for Margaret after that episode, even though it wasn't her fault.

Diabetes is a disease that appears to run in family genes and was generally fatal within a few years during this period in time, as doctors knew little about the treatment and it was difficult, especially for our family, to visit the doctor in those days. Dad's older brother was afflicted with diabetes and died near the beginning of the century at the age of twenty-six. Our older sister suffered with this disease during her teen age years and lived just a few days short of her nineteenth birthday, mainly because the great flood of 1937 inundated all the roads adjacent to the Scioto River, preventing us from obtaining medical help for her. An older brother was to die in his fortieth year of life after having endured this disease for more than twenty years.

Seldom, if ever, did one go to the doctor or dentist unless it was an acute emergency. Various home remedies would be taken to offer relief. Castor oil was the gold standard treatment for most stomach complaints, and it seldom took us youngsters long to learn that the cure was generally worse that the symptoms. Castor oil wasn't a pleasant household name, as it was a measure our parents used to control undesirable activity along with stomach ailments. When one of us became unruly, the threat of a teaspoon of castor oil would immediately have a desired impression on our demeanor. Scratches and cuts were treated with a native balm like hog grease, or when available, an over the-counter salve might do the trick. Salve was useful to rub on the chest when one had a cold, and liniment would soothe our aching muscles. These shelf medicines were believed to have worked in most circumstances, but our budget was tight, and often most of these medicines were beyond our reach. When we came down with chest congestion, homemade poultices of herbs and onions were applied to the chest area to bring relief. Some home poultices consisted of moist and heated meal or clay.

Baking soda was used for toothpaste and our fingers for toothbrushes. Lye soap, a detergent made from the solution obtained by soaking ashes, was the only cleansing product available for sanitation. When lye soap was used in hard water, it offered very little sudsing power and seldom left one's skin as smooth as modern day soaps. Bathing a passel of kids in one old washtub? Maybe once a week! Following our weekly bath and washing of hair, it was desirable to have a little brilliantine to slick our hair down and keep it under control, especially for the older ones who went visiting in the community and had visions of meeting a favorite of the opposite sex.

Most people in our generation grew to adulthood without ever having their eyes examined, and many schoolchildren were believed to be poor students, or were told they would never know anything when their real problem was simply poor vision. Dad was afflicted with vision problems as a young man and had to wear glasses, but they were seldom up-to-date. None of us children had ever had an eye examination while we lived on the hill.

Grandma's reading was primarily that of the Bible and a couple of other religious magazines, and to see the print well enough to read, she wore "store-bought glasses," which were simple magnifying glasses that were encased in frames that only enlarged the print. When she complained that she was having trouble reading, a pair of ten-cent store glasses would be on the shopping list the next time anyone went to the ten-cent store. As she became older she needed double-strength lenses, and at times she wore one pair of glasses over the top of another pair, especially when she was living in her eighties.

One spring morning, just after we had butchered a hog, as our clan was preparing breakfast, an older sibling was frying eggs and bacon—a rarity at our home—in the old iron skillet without the protection of a screen over the skillet. When grease containing small particles of meat is heated to a high degree in an open skillet, it begins to pop and splatter in all directions. Suddenly we heard a searing scream from the vicinity of the cookstove, and responding to the cry for help, we observed our brother covering his face and eyes with his hands, impressing upon the rest of us that he had been blinded with hot grease. Although it must have been very painful at the time and frightening for all of us, it did not appear to be a serious accident, and he was most excited to be excused from school for a few days. Through incidents like this one, we learned early on how to use a little misfortune to our advantage and get sympathy when the daily chores were front and center.

Dad shaved once or twice a week with a straight razor, unless he had planned to make a day trip off the hill. The straight-edged razor is a knife-like instrument having a long blade with a very sharp edge, and for slick shaving, it required honing once in a while. He would lather his face with soap, and after starting to shave, decide that the razor was scratchy. After visiting the leather strap which was hanging from the wall and stroking the razor back and forth on it, all the while testing the cutting edge with his finger until it suited, the shaving process would continue. Incidentally, that old strap had another function. When some of us children became too unruly, it would be removed from its station, and when vigorously applied to the posterior of the guilty one, it quickly got the attention of the offender.

Our water supply was never tested for bacteria, but if it began to taste bad, we would use water from another well until the foul taste cleared up. We kept a bucket of water in the kitchen for drinking, and the old tin cup hanging on the side was used by all members of the family. If perhaps thirsty sojourners ventured by, they would feel at home when taking a drink from that old tin cup. We had been told if water flows at least ten feet over sand and gravel, it would be safe to drink—and we thought it was. While the creeks were flowing, they left small pools of water along the way, and when we were nearby and thirsty we often drank from them instead of going to the house.

When the water reservoir in the cookstove was empty, a large teakettle graced one of the burners to provide hot water when we were cooking. The teakettle was also used to heat water to wash dishes and our hands and faces, and for taking baths, among many other uses when hot water was necessary. Much of the time, we just washed our hands and faces in cold water.

Monday was generally a day for washing our clothes. The clothes to be washed were boiled in a large tub of hot water with homemade detergents. Lye soap was the detergent of choice, and when washing clothes, several slices from a large bar were added to the boiling water. This primitive soap made few suds as the water was hard, permeated with various minerals from the ground. After we scrubbed our clothes on the washboard and thoroughly rinsed them, the small articles would be vigorously squeezed with our hands to get the excess water from the garments. Two of us would twist the larger pieces to ring out as much water as possible before they were hung on a nearby barbed wire fence to dry.

A hand iron was used when more delicate garments needed ironing, but seldom did we bother with ironing as it required the hand iron to be reheated quite often. Ironing was seldom worth the effort as our association with other people in the community didn't require our clothes to be wrinkle-free! During cold winter nights, that old iron was put to a good use. It could be heated, wrapped in a towel, and placed under the blankets to keep our feet warm!

A straw broom for sweeping the floor and old rags tied to the end of a broom stick to made a mop were used to gather up some of the house dust. Discarded pieces of clothing were used for dusting the furniture. These were the only sanitary and cleaning tools we possessed. As both of our stoves used wood for fuel, one can imagine the amount of ash dust that filtered into the air each day, finally coming to rest on the furniture and the floor.

We got a haircut a few times a year, and for sure just before school started in the fall. Our hair was cut short to ensure that we didn't harbor head lice and infect other children with them. When we did get head lice, we used a fine-toothed comb in an attempt to remove them from our hair, this being an everyday job as long as there was any sign of head lice in the family! When conditions became drastic, washing one's hair in a coal oil solution would likely do the trick.

Our clan was certainly an active bunch and we were constantly engaged in commotions that could have easily caused more serious injuries than we suffered. Swinging from grapevines, rolling down the hillsides inside old automobile tires, jumping off steep cliffs and out of the hay mow, working with horses, and wielding sharp tools like the axe and crosscut saw are just a few examples of the goings-on that we were exposed to that could have caused serious injury to our bodies. Fortunately, most of us just incurred occasional bruises and a few minor cuts on our arms and legs.

We probably underestimated the danger of a roaring fire that was necessary to keep our house warm during the winter months. Although the heating stove didn't have protective guards around its sides, we were seldom burned, and those burns were never serious. Many homes were destroyed when excess heat from the flue heated the adjacent wooden frames, causing them to catch on fire. We were most fortunate in all those years that our homes were spared from the ravages of fire, as there was just a thin metal fitting to protect the wood structure where the flue exited the house.

We were reminded of the danger of fire one afternoon when we looked over the hill toward the north and saw a large plume of black smoke rising into the air and filling the valley where our neighbor's home once stood. Injury and damage from house fires were probably the greatest dangers to families living in frontier homes.

7. Getting Around

Traveling long distances was a rarity in those early days, so all we had to contend with was local activity throughout the neighborhood, and that wasn't a big problem with us. Rarely did we venture beyond the rectangular-shaped community between Bear Creek and Camp Creek, an area that measured approximately three miles by four miles. Not having an automobile, like many other families our mode of transportation was simply by "shank's mare," meaning we walked wherever we went. About the only places we would go would be to church, the local grocery store, school, or to visit a relative or a friend. When we needed to go to the grocery store, the items were so few that they could easily be carried home in a sack, although we did ride the horse to the store occasionally. If we traveled on Sunday to see relatives or go to church, we walked, but sometimes piled into the wagon without regard of the horses needing a day of rest. When a family member needed to go to Portsmouth, about eighteen miles down the Scioto River road, he would start walking and hope to catch a ride with a good Samaritan. It was generally safe for persons owning automobiles to pick up hitchhikers along the highway and carry them to their destination, and those of us having a need to visit the city depended on our good neighbors for this service. Regardless of the success of hitching a ride, the trip consumed the entire day and seldom was the journey completed before late evening, and quite often, depending on how much we had to walk between rides, well into the night.

In later years, we patronized the Kroger store at Lucasville as often as possible, although it was seven miles in distance, as the staples in the larger stores were somewhat cheaper than at the local grocery, and the few pennies saved certainly justified the extra time that was consumed to travel the farther route. The fourteen-mile journey began at an early morning hour, and hopefully we would complete our journey before nightfall.

If we realized a return from selling eggs that exceeded the grocery bill, a small slab of bologna might be included in the grocery purchase, and a hunk of that good stuff on a slice of bread made a nice sandwich for weary travelers on the return trip home. On one such trip, an old mangy dog got wind of our delicacy and just wouldn't go home until he got a fair share. After a spell of his trailing the wagon at close range—which bothered no one—it happened that a Model A Ford was traveling in the same direction as we were, and just as it started to pass our wagon, a small part of a bologna sandwich found a resting place directly in front of that old car. That old mangy dog, being as hungry as the passengers on the wagon, darted for the morsel as quick as a flash, which placed him smack dab in front of the speeding vehicle.

Now the Model A Ford, with high ground clearance, and the dog, being low to the ground in an attempt to grab this morsel, paired up to make a perfect combination to exhibit a barrel-rolling effect that left the old dog in a daze and with a desire to get away from our wagon as fast as possible. Dad, who had been looking ahead, inquired as to why the dog was making such a fuss! It isn't remembered if the old dog snatched the morsel before being rolled by that old car, but the young passenger missed his sandwich and the remaining trip home was not all that satisfying to his stomach! Whoever made the fourteen-mile pilgrimage was a tired lot when the time came to bed down for the night.

At the beginning of the forties when Dad was still working on the WPA, he somehow purchased an old Model A Ford sedan, his first automobile. As can be remembered, neither Dad, who at this time was well into his fifties, nor any of us children had ever driven a car before this purchase. Desiring to drive the old Ford home, we reworked the rough spots in the road by filling in the ruts and removing other debris. This didn't require a lot of work because those old Fords could maneuver over rough terrain very well, as they were equipped with tall wheels that helped protect the undercarriage from striking rocks and other high places in the road.

When the road was deemed passable, an older sibling climbed behind the wheel and gave it the gas. Seeing that old car coming over the hill was a memorable experience for us youngsters, and one can imagine that for some time to come we enjoyed the luxury of having a family automobile like many other people, and all of us were pretty much awestruck having our own car to admire. At last, we were now keeping up with the Joneses...er, Smiths!

The older boys were most anxious to learn to drive, and after they'd mastered a few of the bare fundamentals, we youngsters were treated with a short ride. The old Ford was used primarily for going to the store, and especially as a Sunday go-to-meeting car which, when running, was a great improvement over the horse and wagon.

The more cheaply built automobiles of that day didn't have electric starters, but there was a slot in the crankshaft pulley at the front of the engine where a long-shafted crank could be inserted to crank the engine in an attempt to get it started, providing all other instruments and gauges were properly set. This cranking could be a very dangerous procedure, as the engine frequently kicked backward if the spark was improperly set or if the engine didn't start. Whoever was cranking the engine could easily suffer bruises or even a broken arm when the engine kicked, an action that caused the crank to recoil in a counterclockwise motion, possibly striking an arm or leg of the person trying to start the car. Another way to start the old Ford was to let it coast down a steep grade and disengage the clutch, which would cause the engine to turn over and start it running. At times we attempted to push the car to start it, but hand power was too slow, and it was difficult to get up enough speed to get it started.

An unforgettable episode occurred one day when the patriarchal boss in charge, who was then about thirteen years old, decided to get the old jalopy running and presumably take all of us for a ride. The gas valve was turned to a flowing position, the spark moved to the proper setting, and after removing the wheel blocks, down the bank it rolled, but when the clutch was let out, it failed to start. Let's try that again! It failed to start...again! By the time it came to a halt the second time, it was across the little road and precariously close to a steep drop-off near the creek. There wasn't enough room remaining for another attempt, yet it couldn't be left there until Dad came home from work that evening. With the old horse hitched to the rear bumper and all of us kids pushing—except one—the day was salvaged when we finally returned the car to its original station on the upper bank. During this provocative venture, guess who remained behind the wheel to steer the old Ford back in place? Well, it was an important job, and someone with responsibility had to be in charge!

During the early era of the automobile, tires and tubes were in the developmental stage, and they didn't have the quality and workmanship to withstand the moderate forces of speed and the summer heat from the macadam roads. Before any journey began, one must take inventory of the tire tools, hand pump, and tube patching kits, as flat tires were very common and a roadside task of repairing flats had to be considered and frequently executed before the trip was completed.

After one memorable Sunday afternoon visit with a brother who had recently committed himself to the state of matrimony, we encountered a laborious journey home when a loud noise was followed by the rumble of a flat tire, an event that brought us to a sudden halt. We younger ones enjoyed playing on the road and watching other traffic while the more responsible ones were becoming indoctrinated with the fine points of repairing flat tires. After a second such episode on that Sunday afternoon, there was a mild display of ill temper, and a few words uttered by the driver, our oldest brother who was still living with the family, that Dad didn't fancy to hear!

As referred to beforehand, the old Ford was primarily used as our Sunday go-to-meeting car. Dad belonged to a church that was affiliated with a conference having their headquarters in Circleville, Ohio, about fifty miles up the river toward Columbus. Each year the association held a week-long camp meeting, which was brought to a climax on Sunday afternoon. Most members with means to travel longer distances made an attempt to be present on the closing day. Our family at last could be counted among the followers in that group.

On Saturday we prepared a Sunday meal of fried chicken with supporting amenities and lowered the Sunday fare into the well for refrigeration. We then anxiously waited for daylight the next morning to begin our journey to the big meeting, which began with our aunt and uncle leading the way in their old Ford. We youngsters, crowded in the backseat, were overjoyed, anticipating the adventures of the day, when just a few miles on the way, suddenly the front hub of the old Ford began grinding on the macadam road and someone cried that one of the front wheels was running up the road ahead of us. It came to rest in the nearby canal! Apparently, in preparation for the trip, someone rotated the tires and failed to secure the lug nuts on the front wheel. Well, we might have made a mistake, but that didn't mean we didn't know how to improvise! After recovering the wheel from the canal and stealing a lug nut from each of the remaining three wheels, we were soon on our way, and arrived safe and sound in time to attend the morning doings and enjoy our chicken dinner with scores of other families.

Automobiles weren't driven much during the winter months because antifreeze wasn't yet on the market and there was no way to prevent the radiator from freezing.

After the summer season of driving ended, it was a custom to winterize the car by draining the radiator and the motor block, jacking up the car and inserting lifters under the axles to keep the weight of the car off the tires. With warm weather, we hoped to enjoy the luxuries of modern transportation again.

Soon after the forties were ushered in, the public work programs were being terminated and Dad lost his job with the WPA. As one might imagine, the old Ford wasn't very reliable and had now become a liability as it was beyond our financial means to maintain it, so we younger siblings were never exposed to the joys of driving, and our family returned to the former mode of getting around.

After jobs loosened up a little and the older youth began to earn a little money, one of their first purchases was an automobile. The church was recognized as one of the centers of culture, and the church yard was a favorite staging area on Sunday evenings for young lads who owned a car. These sessions gave rise to a lot of boasting about the drivers' skills and their cars' power and speed. This bragging led to frequent challenges to determine each other's racing skills, burning rubber on the nearby road, or spinning gravel in the parking lot.

One night in the early forties, after the normal congregation of several sports, someone bragged about the speed of his car, and it wasn't long before he was roaring up the valley on a road that was routed along a creek having large sycamore trees guarding its banks. This road was much too crooked for racing by young and inexperienced drivers. Besides the driver and another passenger in the first car, a second car followed. The second car returned shortly with news that caused a hush over those who were anxiously waiting in the church yard to hear the outcome of the race. For years when we walked past that big sycamore tree and saw the scars that had been inflicted by that Sunday-night collision, we were reminded of the youthful and inexperienced life that had been lost and the remorse the community experienced from that Sunday night tragedy.

It was desirable to chum with other boys who had an occasional access to their dad's car. In one such instance, several of us Bear Creek boys were invited to go on a joyride to a nearby village—we later believed we enjoyed this pleasure at his father's suggestion—which we accepted. Arriving at our destination and cruising the streets for a few minutes, we passed a gasoline station and were informed that we needed gasoline, and it was suggested that we might pitch in for a few gallons. The ride ended shortly thereafter, with most of our gasoline still in his tank. Although we were subsequently invited to take other rides, we declined the invitation as we were not desirous of being taken a second time, much to his chagrin, and without doubt his father's also.

The farmer who hired us for seasonal work owned one of the first V-8 Fords. His two teenage sons borrowed the car for a Saturday evening, and the three of us motored to a neighboring village with desires of engaging some of the town girls in a few flirtatious moments. Failing in our endeavor to make willing contacts, we left the town with no particular destination in mind. Arriving at an intersection at the edge of the village, a brief disagreement ensued as to which road to take. Without a consensus, the driver—not desiring to take sides—failed to react at the intersection, split the difference, and we came to an abrupt stop, upside down at the bottom of a dry creek bed. What a way to end what we thought was going to be a romantic evening. Years later, an occasional ache from the broken wrist is a reminder of a wasted Saturday night.

A bicycle offered the opportunity to move up in the social status with other teens in the community, and it was the goal of every boy to obtain a nice bike. The first big purchase with money earned from summer work at the nearby farm was a little blue bicycle. It cost twenty dollars, and it took twenty days in the fields cutting weeds and stacking hay to earn that much money, but it was worth it! Those who owned a bike could ride with the crowd and cover much more territory, and occasionally bike to a community a half dozen miles away. It would be a common scene to observe several lads racing up and down the Bear Creek road on a Sunday afternoon.

One sport didn't ride a bike, but did have a nice horse and sulky, and delighted in challenging us bikers to a race. The horse generally won the first few hundred feet, but as the race progressed, a good biker would always make out.

The Bear Creek road, running east and west, was constructed on a steep decline near the junction where it intersected with the state highway that ran north and south, paralleling the Scioto River. One must make a ninety-degree left-hand turn toward the north and ride a couple of miles before reaching our lane. On one return trip from Bear Creek, there were three of us boys and only one bike, but that didn't mean that two were left walking. As we approached the top of the hill near the intersection, it was unanimous that we could make the turn at the bottom—well, it wasn't really discussed, we just hit it!

Three teens on a bike that was built for one person, moving down the hill at a high rate of speed...well, that big turn at the intersection came up on us very quickly, and we didn't make it. A wheel simply collapsed from the pressure of the overload as we turned to the north, and all three of us were tossed across the highway and landed on the berm on the opposite side of the road. Fortunately, except for scrapes and bruises, and not meeting a car as we ran through the intersection, we survived the ordeal, although our dignity was deflated. The bike had to be carried home and undergo extensive reconstruction.

This wreck was not to be the last that this little blue bike would be involved in. One evening, after dark and with only a red reflector on the rear fender for identification, this writer was returning home on the canal road from Camp Creek, and just a few yards from our lane the shadow of the bike and rider was most noticeably in front of the bicycle, warning the rider that a car was directly behind, even though the bicycle was on the berm of the road. Reacting as fast as possible, the little bike moved to the right, but there wasn't enough time to prevent our being struck from the rear. The bicycle was tossed into the air and banged against the guardrail. The passenger, without being hurt, luckily, landed on the grass near the edge of the road. Thankfully the car wasn't going very fast and the only reason for this accident must have been a careless or possibly a drunken driver. The little blue bike didn't fare as well as its rider. It was carried home, and upon examination the next day, it was determined that it couldn't be repaired again. Shoes never lasted as long when walking as they did when having a bike to ride.

8. Frustration and Tragedy

As one can imagine, both our farming equipment and domestic animals were not of premium quality. When the wagon was overloaded, there was danger that a wheel would collapse if the load shifted when on a hillside, resulting in a job of making new spokes before we were back in operation.

A sled was a piece of equipment ill-fitted for most everything except for hauling something when the ground was covered with snow, as it was an implement that had to be dragged both up and down the hills, and for the horses it was work no matter what the terrain. The sled runners—generally made of hickory limbs and curled up at the front end—that would help the sled too more easily pass over rough ground were frequently in need of replacement, as they were dragged on the ground all the time, causing them to wear out quickly. Sometimes, when on a hillside, or if the sled runner struck a large rock, there could be a sudden shift of the load that would tend to crush one of the side runners, giving rise to frequent repairs. It appeared that we were always repairing the equipment, which was time-consuming, and there were days when reconstruction was about all that was accomplished.

Our implements and tools were all quite crude. Most of us fondly remember the monkey wrench, commonly referred to as a knuckle buster. The monkey wrench was a simple tool with adjustable square jaws and was used to tighten, remove or replace the heads on bolts. It was almost impossible to get a good grip on the head of a bolt, and often the atmosphere surrounding the workplace would turn blue with uncomplimentary language when the jaws slipped off the head of the bolt, causing one to bang or bruise his hand against the implement being worked on.

Our beasts of burden were generally secondhand stuff. One old horse was blind, which severely restricted his value as he required constant care. When working in the fields, one of the younger kids was assigned to ride him to prevent his trampling on the crops or falling and hurting himself. Holding the bridle reins tight caused him to hold his head up and raise his front feet a little higher to prevent stumbling when working on rough terrain. While he was a good worker, he could easily be referred to as a typical portrayal of our livestock, farm equipment, the general production of the land, and emblematic of our surroundings in general.

Another horse to be remembered was a young and graceful mare that Dad acquired by going into debt. Soon after we bought her, she became diseased in her neck, possibly by a warble-fly that deposited its eggs under the animal's skin, causing a large growth that seeped continually and made her weak and almost useless. Her successor, a young and strong workhorse, foundered on early spring grass and died within a couple of days, leaving us with an old mule to do the farm work. Jack, the old mule, being crippled in one hind leg, could hardly carry his own weight, and heavy pulling was out of the question for him.

Farmers who had worked and traded horses all of their lives could quickly tell the approximate age of the animal by looking at its teeth. The teeth of a young horse closed together tightly, straight up and down, but as the animal grew older the teeth began to protrude outward and became discolored. Most of our working horses were ones that had long and protruding teeth. They were not nearly as valuable as younger horses, nor did they have the ability to do a hard day's work. A short period of work in the field, especially when pulling a breaking plow, was about all that could be expected of them. Such were the working horses and mules we needed so badly for any work that could not be accomplished by hand.

While the milk cows were of a run-of-the-mill breed, they did provide a welcome and necessary supplement to our diet when they were producing. Cows dry up and don't produce any milk for a couple of months before their calves are born, and when we only had one cow, there would be a dry period lasting a couple of months in which there would be no milk for the table.

We generally kept our animals until they became old and died of natural causes. After finding one in the field that had gone to its happy hunting ground, a postcard would be mailed to the industry that collected dead animal carcasses, requesting the remains to be removed. Three or four days later, we could expect the "dead wagon" to arrive and, with the removal of the carcass, the air in the vicinity would finally be cleansed again. In the era before the dead wagon, deceased animals would simply be dragged deep into the woods where the remains were eaten by wild animals, or simply go back to nature.

There was a young man, big and strong, who lived just across the hill on the Bear Creek road, who worked on the truck that removed such freight for farmers. On one particular call, an insensitive farmer, recognizing the lack of the young man's mental ability, desired to make sport and challenged him to sit on the old animal carcass that had been ripening for several days and eat his lunch. The reward of fifty cents was a goodly sum that represented a couple of hours of work in those days, and he just couldn't pass up such a bargain during those hard times. The lad rightfully earned his due, much to the chagrin of the farmer, but the truck driver refused to let him ride inside the truck on the way back to the processing plant.

Laying hens, like milk cows, went through a dry period, and during those times egg production barely provided for our table needs. When we didn't have eggs to sell, the loss of that small income severely limited the purchase of household necessities. Economically, these setbacks of domestic production presented difficult periods in our lives, and made it impossible for us to become affluent. When we regulated the times when the chicks were to be hatched, we had a better supply of eggs throughout the year.

We children were constantly exposed to various childhood diseases that were aggravating and sometimes life-threatening, such as smallpox, scarlet fever, and mumps. Polio, though this disease was somewhat rare, was life-threatening and most crippling, as there were no vaccinations for the various childhood diseases that inflicted us. All that parents could do in times of sickness would be to provide as much comfort as possible until these diseases ran their course. In the case of two members of our family, the dreaded disease of diabetes was responsible for their demise while they were still young persons.

The extreme political events of the early forties ushered in trying times for our family. The older siblings had left home in an attempt to find work on farms or in industry, but their absence left a void to be filled by the younger ones who were not mature enough to assume the responsibility of running the farm. War clouds were gathering in both Europe and the Far East. Dad, whose health had begun to deteriorate, was approaching sixty years of age, and it became a continual struggle to keep food on the table and provide constructive guidance for us children who remained at home.

Dad at various times affirmed that he was suffering from an upset stomach, but this affliction may have been exacerbated more by heavyheartedness than by a physical ailment, as his health appeared to worsen during those tumultuous years. In keeping with the mores of that age, and because of the economic status of the family, he relied on self-prescribed medical remedies, such as eating wood charcoal and drinking small doses of kerosene. At one time, he even tried smoking field blossom, an aromatic plant that grew in our fields and was believed to have contained some elements of medicinal properties—many of us boys had been in that field before, but not for medicinal remedies—but relief continually evaded him. As he reflected on the dilemma of being lonely by not having a helpmate to share his burdens, we were too young to recognize that he was dealing with both personal and emotional conflicts while working through these difficult times.

It has been said that it becomes a tragedy when parents live longer than their children, and one could say that very few fathers have been visited with a greater occurrence of sorrow than ours. Primary reasons that could be contributed to our family's quandary were the loss of loved ones, economics, and lack of medical care and family planning. There were fifteen children born in our family, with only nine living to adulthood. As the new year started in 1937, Mom and Dad had already lost five children in infancy, but this year marked the beginning of several tragedies with adult members that would occur in the next few years. Our oldest sister, being just short of her nineteenth birthday, succumbed to diabetes in January. She had been fighting that disease for several years, but living off the beaten path and having little access to medical attention, it was very difficult to keep the disease under control. She was unfortunate enough to have a severe reaction to her affliction at the same time the great flood of 1937 occurred, which inundated all of the roads along the river and medical help could not be obtained in time to stabilize her condition.

In 1938, Dad would suffer the loss of his helpmate. Mom was now forty years old, and the time had come for her to deliver her fifteenth child. Complications set in during the time of delivery and neither Mom nor her little boy survived the night.

When death did occur in our neighborhood, it was customary for the undertaker to call at the home and prepare the body for burial. Following this formality, a wreath would be hung on the door to announce the start of a period of mourning, and relatives and neighbors would visit to offer their condolences and attend twenty-four hour vigils that were observed until the time arrived for the burial, which generally took place on the third day. When the day of the funeral arrived, germane to our family, the casket would be carried from the hill by hand, or transported on a wagon to the river road before it was placed it into the hearse and removed to the church house for the last rites. By the time the procession had arrived at the church, it was most likely filled with relatives and neighbors.

Official ceremonies for the last rites of the deceased began with the congregation singing hymns to reflect the destination of the deceased loved one, followed with favorite solos and reflections on the life of the departed. After the presentation of a lengthy dissertation explaining the glorious state where the loved one is already in attendance—seldom was one condemned to the nether world, regardless of their moral standing in the community—amid mournful wailing and sobbing, the formality would finally come to a close and everyone in the church passed by the coffin to view the remains for the last time. The family was the last to pay their respects and some were overwhelmed with grief and remorse. Some family members, in their desire to linger in the presence of their loved one, had to be physically supported as they removed themselves from the church building. After the burial ceremonies, the family would return home...and life would go on.

Following Mom's death, there were six of us children under the age of sixteen. Dad was still working on the WPA and our tribe was left in the care of the oldest sibling still living at home. When Dad came home after work, he supervised the evening chores and helped in planning the next day's activities. As Dad's work was paramount, it was important that a family member shoulder the responsibility for the family's daily affairs. When school started, domestic arrangements were necessary because the youngest member of the family, being just four years of age, wasn't old enough to attend school. This problem was solved by having an older sibling stay at home during school days. While Dad continued to work, the older siblings managed the home front until another became mature enough to be in charge.

As the forties arrived, war clouds hung over the nation and young people became subjected to the armed forces and would likely be deployed to the war zone. At the height of the war in 1943, there were two members of our family who were subject to be drafted into the army. Our oldest brother was called up by the draft board, and after finishing basic training was assigned to an Air Force base in England. In the spring of 1944, his squadron trained for aerial transport duty in preparation for the major offensive on the mainland of Europe, commonly referred to as the Invasion of Normandy. His aerial squadron's main mission was to ferry behind enemy lines glider planes that were loaded with paratroopers, but they also delivered food rations and munitions to the soldiers stationed on the invasion front. Well before daybreak on D-day, his squadron began ferrying glider planes across the English Channel to the mainland of France, and this operation continued to be executed for many days. Apparently, his aircraft had made several successful flights during the first few weeks of the invasion.

In the early summer of 1944, the War Department in Washington shattered the peaceful tranquillity of our lives with news that was feared by thousands of parents whose sons and daughters were in harm's way. Although a similar notice had been previously delivered to numerous parents across America in the same manner, a sad message was now delivered to us. Being a very religious person, Dad no doubt believed his faith would afford him with spiritual strength when experiencing these dark days, but his anguish—along with the recent losses of a daughter and companion—may have left him in the lowest state of despondency that he had experienced in his life.

For our family, military requirements were not yet over. Dad said a tearful goodbye to five sons who were called to duty and served their country during world conflicts in the forties and fifties. However, in 1960 sorrow once again would visit Dad with the loss of his next oldest son, who succumbed to diabetes at the age of forty. Dad was now in his upper seventies, engaged in a third matrimonial relationship with less than pleasant circumstances, and tired. He would live six more years before his labors were finished.

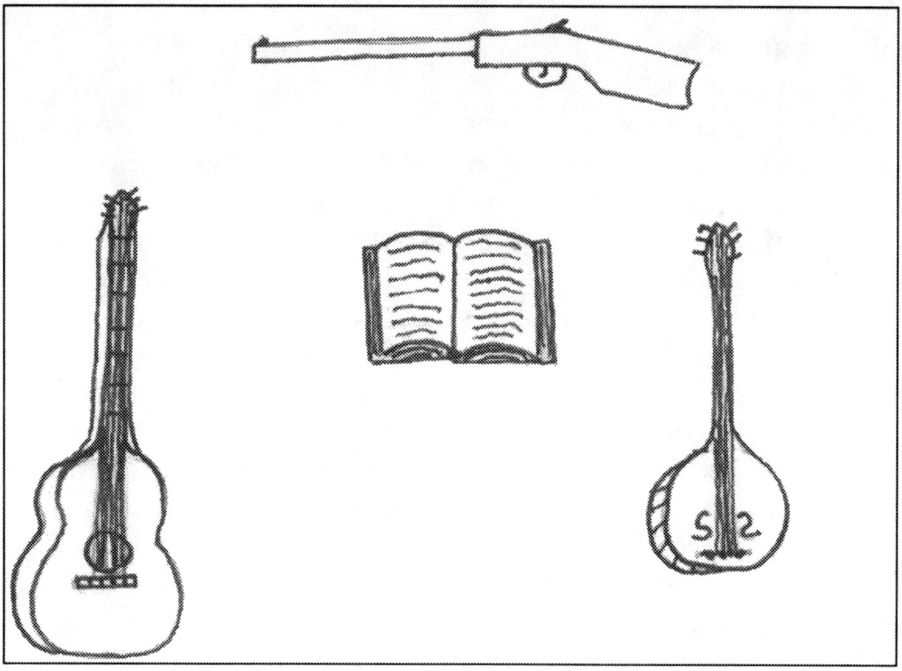

9. Seasons of Refinement

Not all of our energy was expended for the necessities of life. We did have time for sporting games, but our toys were of crude construction since we created them from domestic products using simple tools. Early on, we learned that if we wanted anything to play with, we would have to make it ourselves. One fun game was called tin can hockey. Three or four of us would take an old tin can and a long wooden stick and play a rousing game of hockey on the road by the house, trying to knock the can over a designated line. Part of the pasture field beside our yard, though not very level, was used for a ball diamond. Softballs were made of old rags that were rolled into very tight balls and tied with a string to prevent unraveling.

Our bats were constructed from select tree limbs or discarded boards.

One popular toy we enjoyed was the homemade wagon, used to coast down the many hills on the farm. We began by selecting a nice log from an oak tree that was about a foot in diameter. Using the crosscut saw, we cut sections from a log about two inches thick for the wheels. After removing the bark and shaping the rim of the wheels with a chisel to make them as round as possible, we bored an inch hole through the center of each wheel for the insertion of the axle.

The axles were constructed from short boards and the ends were whittled to size to allow insertion into the holes that were bored in the center of the wheels. The front axle was attached with one bolt to the front of a wide board that was to be used for the bed. This allowed the axle to pivot. The rear axle was fixed, as it was nailed to the bed at several places. Finally, a liberal amount of grease would be applied before the wheels were installed and pinned to the axles. We just pointed the wagon down a hill and away we'd go! Wagons were also used to haul water and wood, among a variety of other uses around the house. With the coming of winter snows, a small sled became a substitute for the wagon and was enjoyed in the sport of sleigh riding.

The automobile tires and tubes had a very short life during the early period of the horseless carriage, especially during the hot summer months when cars were operated on the hot macadam roads. Old tires and tubes that were beyond repair were sometimes discarded along the highway. As we walked along the roads, we confiscated these items for future use. The inner tubes were made of rubber and made good elastic bands for sling shots, a favorite toy. After selecting a good strong Y-shaped wooden fork from a hickory branch, we would cut two rubber bands from the inner tube, each about a foot long, and prepared a pocket made from the remains of an old leather shoe. These three components were assembled with twine string, and when completed, one had a weapon of pride to be carried in the back pocket. A selection of nice round pebbles for ammunition—marbles and walnuts worked well—put the owner in good standing for target practice or to commit other deeds that shouldn't have been executed.

Another slingshot we used inside the house consisted of a large empty spool that had previously stored thread. Again, we cut a small Y-stick and carved two small notches at the top of the rib of the spool to hold a rubber band in place. When using small beans or pebbles for ammunition, you would have a weapon that would get one's attention, especially when accurately directed toward his/her derriere.

A favorite toy enjoyed by the older kids was a whip. We cut a long branch from a small hickory tree, an inch or so in diameter and about ten feet long, and trimmed the small twigs from it. Beginning at the tip end of the pole, we slit the bark into three equal strips, stopping about two feet from the butt end to leave a handle with plenty of leverage. The bark was carefully skinned back to that juncture and the skinned part of the pole was discarded. The three strands of bark were platted very tight and the whip was completed by tying a flexible strip of leather or bark on the whip end to make it crack. When one learned the skill of using the whip, the sound of its cracking would resonate throughout our little valley. One dare not attack with it, as it took little effort to really put hurt on another person. Old-timers kept whips in their hands while working teams of horses, and especially when working a yoke of oxen.

It was fun and easy to make mirrors. We started with a reasonable-sized piece of broken windowpane. After lighting the coal oil lamp, the wick would be turned up in the burner until it gave off a plume of black smoke. By placing the broken glass above to the smoking lamp, one side of the glass would become blackened, and we had a perfect mirror. On a bright and sunny evening, we used it to reflect a beam of light against the western hillside that was now in shadows. We also learned a primitive signal system by flashing the mirror with certain maneuvers.

A particular shape of glass was perfect to pull pranks on each other. A magnifying glass held just an inch or so from one's body part, and at the proper angle in relation to the sun, would focus a very hot sun spot in a small area, causing the offended person to take revenge when the shoe was on the other foot. When the grass was dry, one could start a small grass fire and watch the smoke curl into the air.

During the winter evenings, our favorite game at home was checkers. We drew a checkered pattern on the side of a cardboard box and used white and yellowed grains of corn for the checkers, engaging in friendly competitions that developed skills, promoted decision making, and at times initiated heated arguments that were cooled when Dad confiscated the checkerboard. One brother liked to brag that he had beaten the community champion while still in his teens, but it can't be remembered that he won any games with his older siblings.

For thrills, one could find a grapevine hanging from a tall tree, preferably one standing near a steep bank, where we could swing over a creek, drop into the water, and splash! We cut the vine near its root, and presto, we had a natural swing for many moments of pleasure. Remembering swings, we generally had one or two tied from the branches of the two large oak trees located near a little creek just to the east of our house. Many hours were enjoyed in those swings while we were growing through those formidable years! Other games included shooting marbles, jumping rope, and pole-vaulting, using a hickory pole and springing from the kitchen patio.

Children playing on dirt surfaces not only get their hands, faces, and bodies dirty, they often put their fingers in their mouths. While this was not always unhealthy, it did present a possible problem that must be dealt with. When kids play a lot in dirt, they are likely to ingest parasites which grow into tapeworms that live in their intestines. Sometime in midsummer, we began to itch in the stomach and lower back area, a symptom requiring medical attention...a tablespoon of castor oil. This was a sizeable dosage of an undesirable remedy that required us to hold our noses tightly until the medicine had gone down. While the cure was undesirable, it would usually bring relief. Although there appeared to be some positive health benefits in these occurrences, they did make ones innards feel tingly.

A hide-and-seek game was a favorite to be played as twilight turned to darkness. The whippoorwill was singing her last song of the evening, the chimney swallows were twitting through the sky for one last tidbit before bedtime, and the crickets began an hour-long songfest to wake up the nocturnal creatures when we began to get involved in this twilight game. We enjoyed it most when our female cousins who were young, vibrant, and pretty were visiting. Generally the younger ones would be "it"—the chasers—and were assigned to search the surroundings for the older ones who had scampered into the nearby bushes and beyond. We generally had a difficult time finding them, and when we found a boy and girl together, they were quite put out when they were come upon! We younger ones got revenge by asking if they were kissing cousins!

The older ones would coerce us younger kids with a big tale to go snipe hunting. After being led a good distance from the house after dark, two of us youngsters were assigned to hold the bag and catch the snipes. The older ones, with sticks in hand and pleading for the snipes to obey them, circled us, thrashing the surrounding meadow in an attempt to herd the snipes toward our bag. While questioning how many we had bagged, they continued to make larger and larger circles until the ones who were holding the bag could no longer hear them. Finally, after the instigators had a big laugh, the ones holding the bag would be rescued and had been taught another lesson in life.

We Bear Creek boys loved to swim in the Girl Scout swimming pool. It was an amenity on a private campground for young girls from Portsmouth who were farmed out by their parents for a couple weeks each summer. Among other activities, they enjoyed daily frolics in the pool that was situated in an isolated area on a flat well below the camp. By frequenting the nearby wooded area, we enjoyed watching the girls frolic alongside the edge of the pool, and we soon learned the hours when the pool was not being used. During evenings when the pool was vacant, we sneaked into camp for a most enjoyable swimming session—in our birthday bathing suit.

Swimming in a nice pool was one of the more pleasurable treats a country boy could imagine, especially on a hot summer evening after working all day in the fields, and we didn't have to take a bath in the old washtub when we came home! Very few weekend afternoons passed without us Bear Creek boys making our way to the pool and having fun during the swimming season.

We always kept our clothes at the edge of the creek, about fifty yards distance, for a quick getaway if some camp official decided we had enjoyed the pool long enough. Hearing an automobile making its way down the graveled road from the camp above prompted us to scamper into the woods before the authorities arrived. We also had to keep a close lookout in the direction of the creek to ensure that none of the more rowdy members in the community would sneak along the bank and make off with our clothes, leaving us in an embarrassing predicament!

We were careful not to do mischief at the pool, and the officials were quite tolerant of us as long as we didn't interfere with their programs. While we frequently enjoyed the swimming holes in Bear Creek itself, they didn't compare to the pleasure of stealing an hour of bliss in that beautiful pool!

While our family was rarely involved, we did become acquainted with the sport of fox hunting. Fox hunting was mostly a weekend sport where the hunters would take their hounds to heavily wooded areas where previous hunting had been successful. The range behind our home fit the bill. Men of this sport prized their fox hounds and cared for them like family. In relation to the economic conditions of that day, serious fox hunters spent a considerable amount of money to acquire and train the finest dogs they could afford.

Generally, on a Saturday night, the local fox hunters selected a sight near the top of the large range of hills to the west of our house. A roaring fire would be built and the hunters would settle in for a long night of hunting. This area was a favorite because it was one of the highest spots in the vicinity, and the hounds could be heard from all directions and for long distances while chasing the fox. It was not desirous for the hounds to catch the fox...just run and bark until both the dogs and the fox were so tired that they called it a draw—nearly daylight the next morning.

Disagreements were frequent in determining whose dog

was leading the chase when the fox was being pressed. Economic conditions prevented the ante from being too large, which just left bragging rights as to who had the best dog during the run. After the contents of a pint of "white lightening" had been consumed and the wee hours of the morning were approaching, the overriding factor was to call in their dogs, go home and perform the domestic chores—and go to bed!

Fox hunting wasn't enjoyed by everyone. Most rural families relied on a flock of chickens for meat, eggs, and spending money. Foxes were predators, and when they raided the chicken house, several valuable hens most likely would be destroyed. We were always on the lookout for these varmints and would never give them a second chance to raid the chicken house. In the mind of the fox hunter, the more foxes, the better the hunt, and they didn't want anyone to kill the foxes, thus bringing the hunter and the homeowner into a conflict, but we did try to get along.

Fox hunters from outside areas hunted our woods without permission and occasionally would lose track of their dogs. The hunters returned for the next day or so in an attempt to find them, but seldom offered a reward, and we didn't have any real reason to cooperate with them. Since the fox wasn't our friend, we weren't very sympathetic toward the hunters, and it has been known that some hunters never did find their dogs. Regardless of whose dog was running the fox, if the fox got caught in the line of fire of that old shotgun, that would be the end of that fox chase. The boom of the old shotgun followed by the silence of the dogs brought forth a bellowing language that would be unfit to print in most publications.

We seldom kept a dog at our house, as most pets were fed with table scraps, and we didn't have food beyond the family's needs. One dog to be remembered was Jack, a medium-sized mixed-breed that wasn't much good for anything. We didn't need a watchdog where we lived, and he didn't care to hunt, but he was fun to play with. One hot summer afternoon, one of the older boys tied Jack to a tree because he had been displaying signs of ill temper, and eventually he began frothing from his mouth. As the day wore on he became very aggressive and was quite wild in his demeanor. We children had been warned to be wary of animals when they were acting strange, and in this instance, the older members of the family knew that Jack had been in contact with another animal and had been inflicted with rabies, a very contagious disease both for humans and animals. With a rifle in hand, they led Jack into the woods, and we never saw him again.

Most families kept dogs for hunting or security. Our neighbor at the end of the lane was the owner of a large German Shepherd that appeared as ferocious as a mountain lion, especially in the presence of us young children. He regularly guarded his territory and would bound toward people from his uphill perch, intimidating them as though they were trespassing on his turf. He threatened people who were walking along the road, or approached members of our family in an aggressive manner as we started up the lane toward home. It didn't take much of his aggressive action to get old, especially when we young children were afraid we might be attacked. Not being strong enough to defend ourselves, we scurried up the lane as fast as possible to get away from this confrontation.

We had to live with the situation…for a while, anyway. That old dog had a weakness—he liked to roam the countryside—and one day he was found along the road a mile or so from home, dead. No one ever took credit for the old dog's demise, but there was some talk that he was ranging along a sparsely settled country road and happened to meet his match with someone who carried a revolver, and that old dog lost out to technology! Whatever, the situation was remedied!

A middle-aged couple who lived about a half mile down the river road that we traveled frequently, owned a large German Shepherd dog that displayed a violent temperament. As pedestrians approached the corner of their yard, they would experience a hair-raising confrontation as that old dog bounded along the fence and put up such an offense that made one wish they could have taken another route. Even thought their yard was enclosed with a woven wire fence, and while no one ever claimed the dog made an attempt to cross it, that didn't make us feel any better as we felt that we were being harassed nearly every time we walked along the road. Along with a buddy who lived near the area where our road joined the highway, it was decided that we had had enough of these harrowing experiences, and we planned a sumptuous treat for the old dog the next Sunday afternoon. Somehow his parents got wind of this escapade and didn't think that it would be proper to embellish the neighbor's dog with a deluxe sandwich that included rat poison, small bits of broken glass, and numerous stick pins. Our mischief had been foiled for the present, but that old dog's days were numbered.

Halloween was the time for big doings for some of us "rowdy-abouts" during those tempestuous years. Young people of all generations have participated in pulling pranks on the older folks, and we were no different. A farmer looking out his kitchen window the morning after Halloween might see a shock of corn in the middle of the road, or a couple of wagon wheels tied high in the opening of his hay mow. A neighbor might run to the outhouse during the wee hours of the morning and discover that it no longer stood upright. A traveler coming home after dark might have to stop a few times to clear the road of debris—and replace it behind his vehicle to the dismay of the next passerby. Rarely would one be so mischievous to stealthily ascend to the top of a neighbor's house and cover his chimney with a board after he had stoked a roaring fire and settled down to enjoy his favorite programs on the radio.

A common Halloween trick, and a very old one, has for ages been played on people who lived in the rural Appalachians, and made a good prank to pull on a neighbor. A family that lived on Bear Creek was headed up by a patriarch whom some in the community referred to as Dag-goon, as this was his byword when he was engaged in conversation. One Halloween, so it has been told, a couple of rowdy boys decided to play a trick on Dag-goon. After scooping up a couple of fresh cow patties, putting them in an old grocery sack and topping them off with dry grass, they quietly stole upon his front porch after darkness had set in, placed the sack that included the cow patties in front of the living room door, set it ablaze, yelled, "Fire!"...and ran to the nearby woods to hide and watch the unfolding response. Well, Dag-goon, a likeable and mild-mannered man, rose from his chair in his stocking feet, hit the door on the run, saw the blaze on the porch, and began stamping out the fire! The perpetrators could only watch, as any reaction to immediate pleasure would reveal their hiding place, and they certainly didn't want to get caught in the act. Whether or not Dag-goon got back in the house that night, it has never been told.

Most youngsters desired to satisfy their curiosity when observing older people smoke or maybe drinking a little. During those days, all smokes were enjoyed by puffing a pipe or a roll-your-own cigarette, which required a few pennies to purchase those fine accouterments, but those of us without monetary means soon learned to improvise. Corn silks began to mature in the middle of the summer, and by rolling the silks into a piece of paper from a brown grocery bag, we made our own cigarettes and pleasured ourselves as if we had the leading store brands. One Sunday afternoon, two of us boys entered the small grocery store at the mouth of Bear Creek and engaged the old storekeeper in a light conversation, with pretense of purchasing some small item. Not having any money between us, we eventually left the store without a purchase, but once we were beyond the bend of the river, we rolled and smoked our cigarettes from a package of loose tobacco that had been confiscated from the tobacco shelf in the store. As we walked up the road, taking pleasure with our ill-gotten gain, the joy began to disappear when we took stock of what we had done. We were afraid to return to the store and face our situation, but the thought of the old storekeeper and friend probably knowing what we had done to him made the situation even worse. Nothing was ever said concerning the incident, and we never mentioned it between ourselves thereafter.

As we became older, we became curious about the forbidden pleasures that adults enjoyed when they were drinking alcohol, even though they sometimes acted strange and boisterous. Most rural people planted small orchards for fruit, with apples being favored. Apples could be grown most everywhere, and several trees often produced more than the family could use for eating and canning, allowing the remainder to be squeezed into juice to make vinegar and apple cider. Apple cider, when preserved correctly, fermented and produced an alcoholic beverage called apple jack, commonly referred to as "a poor man's drink." When young boys stole into the cellar where apple jack was stored, school didn't mean very much the next day!

Fifteen Kids
and
an Old Blind Horse

The Prohibition Act of the twenties opened the door for thousands of hill farmers to turn their corn into whiskey, from which they could realize a much greater return than if they sold their corn at the grain market. While making whiskey was illegal, the money derived from illegal spirits made in the local stills provided an income for a few of the huge number of people suffering unemployment. Fathers who would never have indulged in this activity prior to suffering from long-term unemployment were now engaged in acts of federal resistance, participating in an illicit endeavor they deemed necessary to provide for their families. Even though money was tight, it was much easier to sell whiskey than it was to sell corn...and a lot more profitable.

People who were engaged in this type of commerce were always on the lookout for revenuers. These federal agents were sworn to uphold the law and rid the land of illegal spirits as Big Uncle deplored the thought of us poor country folk engaging in a few social nips that might bring some enjoyment into our lives. One Sunday morning in early summer, this writer ventured toward Bear Creek on the eastern path from home and was startled when he heard several people crashing through the woods in the distance. After moving a little closer to the interference, he came upon a contraption having various containers, or vats, and a large coil of copper tubing. This was a sudden encounter, and, after approaching the site, it was understandable why he had heard the footsteps of persons scampering through the trees to get out of sight. There was really no reason to be alarmed as the perpetrators fled just to protect their identity. If all progressed well, one might have explored the nearby creek a few days hence and discovered a still that was surrounded with brush to camouflage the site.

When making country whiskey, a boiling pot was filled

with corn mash, and when sugar and a package of yeast were added, the fermenting process would begin. Following a determined time for leavening, heat would be administered to the vat and cause the solution to boil, forcing the steam through cooling tubes where it condensed into liquid. The distillation procedure was generally performed during the night to hide any smoke that may escape and reveal the secret location of the still. Thus, a product with a slang name of "moonshine" was born. The finished product looked like water, but its content of alcohol was very high. Most people favored a spirit that had some coloring, and not a few distillers tried to please their customers by soaking or boiling reddish tinted cloths, like an old red work shirt, or adding a small amount of artificial coloring into the mix. These gray procedures often caused the mix to become contaminated, and many cases of whiskey poisoning occurred to the sorrow of the consumers. Regardless of the color, when it was consumed as a beverage, well, it would kick, and one would always remember his first drink of "white lightening"! At fifty cents a pint, one could have a long weekend and a sorry Monday morning!

A still might cause problems among moonshiners who produced the spirits and bandits who desired to make a raid when the finished product was ready to be drawn. Those who were engaged in the production of these spirits were desirous of protecting their turf and it was dangerous for an outsider to be caught in the vicinity of a manufacturing plant when the moonshine was in the stage of being siphoned and bottled. Seldom would moonshiners venture into the heavily forested areas without weapons to protect themselves and their investment. A good watchdog, one that warned its master by growling rather than barking, was a necessity, allowing time for the moonshiners to escape if they were being hunted by the revenuers, or prepare to protect their site from those who might desire to raid their still.

When distillers produced more spirits than the local trade would bear, they sold their product to "rum runners," carriers who drove fast cars and transported the illegal whiskey to large cities where it was in demand. The illegal whiskey industry became so lucrative that organized crime gained control of retail operations, and under mob rule became a scourge in our large cities.

Speakeasies, underground centers of nightlife where people could party and drink illicit liquors, surfaced throughout the nation during the period of prohibition. Women began to accompany their escorts and frequent those houses of ill repute quite regularly during the roaring twenties. Musical bands were engaged for entertainment and the speakeasy guests enjoyed an evening of drinking and dancing. These club dances that originated during the prohibition years were lively and entertaining, and their popularity gave rise to a vigorous nightlife atmosphere, along with a new genre of pop culture. Many of the big bands of the thirties and forties were born during the prohibition movement.

The local farmer for whom some of us worked was one who imbibed on strong drink when the opportunity presented itself, which was quite often. One Saturday afternoon we went to the bottoms to plow corn. He had a bottle of wine on the tractor and as we continued to nip from the jug, plowing corn became less and less important. It just happened that Dad had been to the grocery store about two miles down the road and was returning home in the middle of the afternoon while we were performing most unusual antics for ones who were working in the corn field. The next day, Dad informed me that as he drove by in the wagon, he observed a couple of people making fools of themselves, staggering around in the edge of the cornfield. No response offered, no apology required. He must have thought that the hangover was adequate punishment.

The home of a favorite cousin who lived in the Sedan area was the scene of many memorable and enjoyable weekend. Two of us boys, one her younger brother, were visiting their home one summer weekend. This particular Saturday afternoon, her husband decided to take us to Portsmouth to do a little sightseeing. Having spent most of our meager funds, it was thought to be appropriate if we took home a fifth of whiskey to entertainment ourselves over the weekend. Having completed the chores and enjoyed the evening meal, it was time to sit back and enjoy a few nips from that bottle of spirits. Her husband kept warning us youngsters that we needed to go easy on that "stuff" to keep from getting sick. We got along quite well under more mature supervision, and the evening ended when we all went to bed in a jocular mood.

The next day, the family had scheduled a visit with her husband's parents, leaving us two lads to care for the homestead. It wasn't very long until we had determined that a large amount of whiskey was still in the bottle. It surely wouldn't hurt to take a nip or two, even though we had been encouraged not to drink anything until he had returned home so that we could all enjoy the evening together. But one little nip wouldn't hurt, or so we told each other. It wasn't very long until we got up enough nerve to take another, and soon we were in a nipping and singing mood that lasted all afternoon and can still be remembered. Our favorite theme that afternoon was "rye whiskey," and how happy we would be if a river was whiskey and we were nearby, we'd swim to the bottom and stay till we died! Our hosts came home later in the evening and found two lads on the floor in the living room. The bottle was empty, the songs no longer had any spirit to them, and suppertime never did come around. The conversation of the evening was nearly mute, and neither of us wanted to remember how we felt as we rose early the next morning and headed for home like whelps with their tails tucked between their legs after they had been whipped.

10. School Daze

The only educational facility in our neighborhood during the early part of the century was a one-room school near the mouth of Bear Creek, attended by the older members of the family and accessible from the hill by the eastern path to Bear Creek. It was about a two-mile walk each way. Neighborhood students attended that one-room school until it was abandoned in the mid-thirties. Districts with a one-room school hired a teacher whose responsibilities often included the custodial care of the building. Children in grades one through eight made up the school enrollment. The building was heated with a pot-bellied stove, and during very cold days, classes were conducted with students seated around or near the stove to keep warm. Drinking water, drawn from the nearby well, was carried into the school house in a galvanized bucket and placed on a small table, and all students used a common tin cup when they were thirsty. When outside and drinking at the well, they mostly formed a cup with their hands, instead of waiting in line to use the tin cup that was attached to the pump with bailing wire. Lunches were prepared at home, and generally consisted of cold bean sandwiches, peanut butter and jelly when available, or maybe a fried egg on a piece of "pone" bread. An apple or peach might round out the fare when those items were available. Lunches were carried to school in brown paper bags. Thus, the term "brown-bagging" was used frequently and became an ordinary saying at lunchtime. A small outhouse was situated on each side of the schoolhouse, one for boys and the other for girls, and hopefully too many children wouldn't have an emergency at the same time.

Activities on the small playground included tag, hopscotch, marbles, and a little softball, using rag balls and sometimes a board bat. The main subjects in the curriculum were the three R's, but upper grade students studied geography, some science, and physics. Discipline was generally strict, but the few boys who didn't pass their grades every year might become a challenge, as they were older and more difficult to discipline, especially for young female teachers. Differences between rival students that weren't settled on the school ground frequently spilled over after school and were settled on the way home. These extracurricular activities, when reported, presented the teacher with more problems the next day, and if the problems remained unsolved the parents would become involved, which most students frowned upon. The general slogan of that day was that if one got a spanking at school, another one would be handed out at home.

The township was eventually consolidated and the school board built a brand new six-room school building on upper Bear Creek. Consolidation meant that children would have to travel a much longer distance to go to school, and to alleviate this problem, school buses were purchased by local entrepreneurs who contracted with the school boards to transport children to school from outlying areas. Buses of that day were not as mechanically reliable as they are today, and many times failed to operate on schedule. This caused children who didn't live close to the road to have long waiting periods at the bus stop. In our situation, there were students from several families who had to walk quite a distance from their homes before they arrived at the bus stop, and we all experienced a lot of waiting.

At our particular stop, we were just a few yards from the Scioto River, and many mornings when the bus was running behind schedule, we played along the riverbank, throwing flat stones on the water in an attempt to skip them across the river. Eventually a shelter house was constructed where we waited to afford protection during inclement weather. Inside this little shanty was the scene of many disagreements, as friction among children of this age surfaces quite frequently.

Adjacent to the shelter house was a large concrete culvert that had been installed under a new section of the highway and controlled the creek that drained our farm land, a mile in the hills. When the weather was very cold, and if the culvert was dry, we climbed down its banks and waited underground until we heard the bus coming up the canal road. The culvert provided much more protection from the cold and inclement weather than did the shelter house.

School was quite different from the modern ones of today, whether a one-room or a six-room building. There wasn't any electrical power in the buildings in those days, and with just a few windows along the outside wall of each classroom, it could get quite dark inside the classrooms on a cloudy day. The buildings were heated with coal-fired stoves or furnaces, and without fans to force the air into the classrooms, the rooms only received the warm air that gravitated into the classrooms through heat ducts. Those rooms near or situated over the furnace room might be quite comfortable, and sometimes hot, but in rooms farthest from the furnace, the children might need to wear their coats to keep warm.

The curriculum in the larger schools was more diverse than it was in one-room schoolhouses, but it was still much more basic than that of today. Classes lasted up to an hour and students were required to stand by their desks—which were fastened to the floor in straight rows—and recite poems, the spelling list for the week, and their multiplication tables. In the upper grades, we were required to memorize the names of our presidents, our states, important rivers, lakes, mountains, or other geographical points of importance, in addition to other pertinent facts that the teacher felt were important. One never forgets Paul Revere's famous ride, selections from various poems that the teacher loved, and always, in the upper grades, Lincoln's famous speech at Gettysburg. Failure to properly recite the assigned lessons was a good cause to get one of your body parts whacked with a ruler!

The tops of our desks were fastened with hinges near the front and could be raised, revealing a storage area for books and other personal items. An inkwell was located at the front of the desktop to hold our ink bottles, a needed item, as we were taught the fine art of using ink to do much of our class work. After the pen point was dipped into the ink bottle to load it, several words could be written before another refill was needed. Some subjects, especially writing, were always written in ink, so we soon learned not to spill the contents of the newly filled pen on our paper as we would be required to start over again. No messy work!

For some, the inkwell had a downside. Girls whose hair was bradded in pigtails or ponytails might lean back too far and later discover that their blond curls mysteriously began to grow black at the ends, initiating another confrontation with the teacher.

The fountain pen, a marvelous invention having a rubber bladder inside its housing to hold a small reservoir of ink, provided continuous writing without the need of being filled too often. One could determine the quantity of ink in the pen's reservoir by pulling a small handle out from the side which depressed the bladder inside the pen. When the bladder was nearly full and pointed toward a nearby student...this was another cause to get one's face slapped and to stand in the corner the rest of the day.

Our grades were recorded in numerical values before the final letter grade was assigned for the grading period, and a value below seventy meant failure. When the scores were translated into alphabetical values, E was excellent; F meant fair, and P was failure. Conduct grades were downers. There were a lot of grade cards that were never taken home, which required the offending students to forge their parent's signature. These acts of deception were generally headed off before too many grading periods passed, and the culprits quickly learned that fraudulence wasn't the answer to poor grades.

There was no such thing as a cafeteria during those early years of school, but by the mid-forties the government became involved in the local needs of the school system and built cafeterias adjacent to the school building, with most or all of the essentials and foodstuffs furnished by the government. Those who ate lunches in the first cafeterias fondly remember cooked cabbage, beans, and soup of the day, which was a concoction of beans, cabbage, tomatoes, and small amounts of meat. The comfort stations were located a couple hundred feet downwind—depending which way the wind was blowing—from the school building, and during the winter months one would refrain from making a pit stop unless relief was urgent. During warmer weather, a personal necessity was always a good excuse to get out of class. Sometimes too much loitering behind the courtesy wall would arouse the attention of our teacher, and we would just have to wait until recess for future relief periods. It is good that young people have strong kidneys! We didn't have running water at the outhouses, and washing our hands following such visits was out of the question, and probably was never even thought about.

Our drinking water was drawn from a well having a modern mechanical pump that was located just a few yards from the school building. Generally, one student would work the pump handle while others drank from a cup formed with their hands. Holding one's hand tightly against the mouth of the pump while a buddy pumped the handle vigorously would broadcast a nice spray of cold water in all directions, causing those nearby to scamper to keep from getting wet.

The beginning of the school year was a release from the dreary and tiresome hot summers on the hill. While many of the academic subjects were interesting, recess was a favorite period. We boys were fiercely competitive in school sports, especially when playing contact games like Blackman and wrestling, but those games were rough and often destructive to our clothing. Shooting marbles was an art, and a good shooter would carry a pocket full of marbles home most every evening.

We had a young man for a principal, quite athletic, who played softball with us during the noon hour, and many of us considered him to be a role model. The previous principal, a much older man, enjoyed his dinner hour in his car, which was parked at the front of the school building where students weren't permitted. Some believed he indulged in habits that we children shouldn't take part in.

The young principal let everyone know where they stood, and school discipline was strict but fair. In those days, an appointment with the principal meant that you were in trouble, and a trip or two to his office would prompt one to straighten up fast or suffer the consequences. An incident that happened on the last day of school one year is worthy of recall. We were scheduled to play an afternoon softball game with a neighboring school, but some of us players had beforehand decided to explore the creek, located on private property and reachable by a path that meandered through a copse of woods situated alongside the playground where the softball diamond was located. This being the last day of school, we were led to believe that we wouldn't be punished, and all would have been forgotten by the time school started in the fall.

When the ballplayers failed to show for the pre-game warm-up, the principal came looking for us...with a switch in his hand that he had cut from a nearby bush. After a few well-placed offensive strikes, we scurried to our positions on the field, with you-know-who behind the batter's plate. As the principal was our school's pitcher, this catcher was constantly reminded that life had to be faced head-on as he faced him all afternoon. A trip to the principal's office would have been preferable.

After the school cafeteria was built, one of the common items served for lunch was cabbage. One fellow called big John loved his cabbage, and after being served his favorite dish, he would often hit the softball against the side of the schoolhouse where many windows were situated, more than two hundred feet from home plate, causing the janitor to perform extra duty by replacing a broken window before going home that evening.

The cook planned to have cabbage for lunch—we were served a lot of cabbage in those early cafeterias—when she knew we were going to play a softball game with the neighboring school. Each time big John came to bat, the students yelled "cabbage, cabbage, cabbage," hoping he would hit a home run or break another window pane. Those game days were certainly fun, as all of the students and teachers in the school would sit along the base lines, rooting for their team and enjoying the afternoon in the sun.

After we had gone on to high school, this young principal always invited us back for the annual "softball alumnus game," and we high school students were treated to a fun afternoon. We alumni were older and wiser, but seldom won the game as we were always outcoached and outplayed. He enjoyed playing his younger squad against us older lads and winning before his school.

Smaller local school districts of that day didn't have the resources or enrollment to justify building high schools, and those desiring to attend high school—many students just finished the eighth grade in rural America during this period—were bussed to the high school at Rarden, a village about ten miles west of the Morgan Township school. By the mid-forties, a greater number of boys and girls began to attend high school as the sixteen-year-old age law was being enforced. Later on, our local school board contracted for the district's high school students to attend a larger school at Lucasville, which was much better situated for our populace and afforded more opportunities for the students.

One of the more enjoyable extracurricular activities at high school was a gun club, sponsored by the teacher who taught the art of woodworking. He organized this club for upperclassmen, and its members enjoyed a shooting contest about once a month. We didn't have second thoughts about bringing our rifles to school on the bus, walking into the school building amongst scores of students and teachers, and placing them in the corner in our manual training room where they remained until we held our shooting contest that evening. Ten or twelve teenagers entering a school building with rifles in hand today would bring out the National Guard! We also carried knives!

Our main bus route ran along the state route west of the Scioto River in a northerly direction from Lucasville, and several of the students in Morgan Township lived on county or township roads that intersected with the main road. At the mouth of the Big Run road there was a small grocery store, and before the bus ran the route on that side road, the driver would slow down enough for some of us lads to jump off to visit the store. These ten-minute round trips allowed us to grab a smoke and purchase a small amenity—if we had any change—before boarding the bus to go on home.

Once in a great while, if we knew there would be a good western at the old Garden Theater in Portsmouth, a couple of us boys would jump off of the bus at the first street corner when we arrived at Lucasville, on the morning run, and hitch a ride to town. Having very little pocket money, we frequented the Play House on

Chillicothe Street, an establishment representing a sports palace that had a bar where drinks and foods were served, several pool tables, and a small bowling alley in the basement. The manager of this facility would allow us to set pins for an occasional bowler, and we might earn enough money to buy a bowl of bean soup for lunch, admission to the theater, and fare for a ticket to ride the bus to Lucasville. Often we were too late to ride home on the school bus and would hitchhike the remaining seven miles.

In the decade of the forties, the "in thing" for most teenagers was smoking, and it was common for students who smoked to carry cigarettes on their person. After having a ten-cent hamburger at the little corner restaurant across the street from the high school, many of us would light up a cigarette before returning to class.

Just before dismissal, some of us skipped the formality of returning to our home room following the last class period and scampered across the street to smoke before boarding the bus to go home. The principal quickly caught on. One evening during our senior year, the above formality was being abused, and when a couple of students were about to crash the door, the scholarly taskmaster was standing nearby, and offered a stern declaration that graduation would be put on hold should this conduct continue. We all graduated!

Higher education was almost unheard of in rural Scioto County, partly because the nearest institution of higher learning was more than fifty miles away, but mostly because students just didn't have the opportunity to further their educations unless their parents were financially capable of sending them to college. This writer graduated from high school in the late forties, and from a class of nearly fifty students, only five won a degree in higher education. However, many young people of that era did take advantage of technical training and contributed greatly to society with their skills and talents.

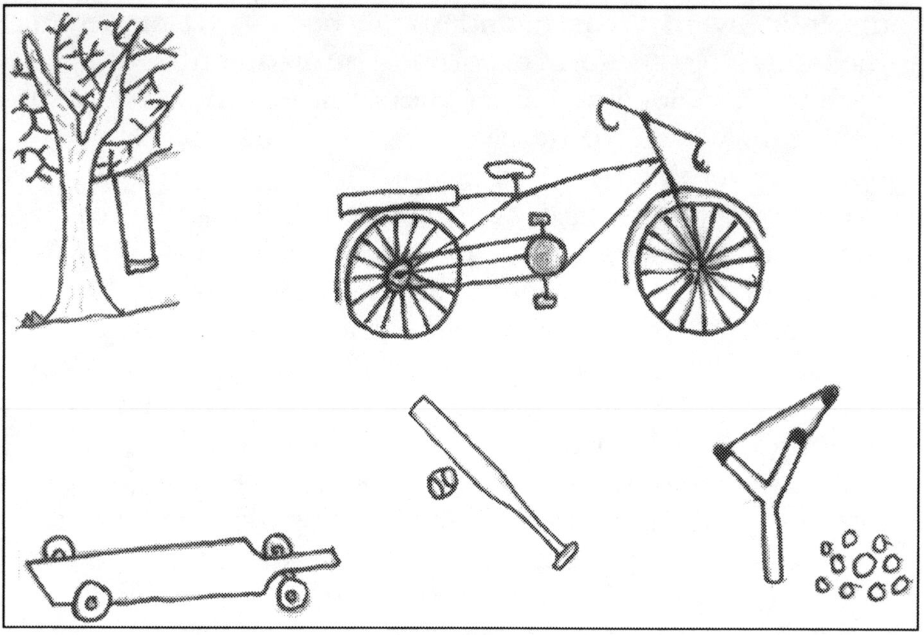

11. Rural Culture

The church was the social center of the lives of frontier people, and Sunday was acknowledged as the big day of the week to go to church to renew old acquaintances and meet new friends. In addition, it was desirable that we become indoctrinated with a strict dose of moral conduct. One of the religious mores of the day, inherited from our ancestors, included attending the house of worship on a weekly basis. An aunt recently told us that Mother just loved to go to church and attended their doings as often as possible, and revealed that their lives revolved around the activities of the church. There is no doubt that all members of our family and community were affected by the teachings of the church. Moral issues and personal discipline were stressed, and unruly deeds were nipped in the bud with some form of corporal punishment. Our lives were to be molded by personal discipline, and we were to adhere to a strict code of ethics that was restrictive in nature and difficult to practice.

Participating in regular church attendance and its other functions apparently had other outcomes, both directly and indirectly. While open dating was frowned upon, especially by the girl's parents, the church provided a mutual meeting place for boys and girls to form relationships—under the watchful eye of the girl's parents. If the lady found a possible suitor who attended church, he may be invited to her home for dinner and enjoy the afternoon with the family. This visitation gave the parents time to scrutinize the qualities of their daughter's young suitor. Following the normal Sabbath activities, everyone returned to church for the evening services, and the young people would part company until the next Sunday. Eventually it was hoped that these controlled romantic relationships would end with the community celebrating the young couple's bond in matrimony.

When living on the hill, we were more or less isolated from society, both physically and culturally. The print material on hand consisted of an old Bible and a Sears Roebuck catalogue. Our knowledge of the outside world, especially current events, was quite limited. Schools didn't offer such amenities as daily newsprint, current events, or libraries, and the only formal materials were old textbooks. In high school we swapped comic books amongst ourselves, and a favorite genre was that of a western setting by famous western authors who wrote stories about life on the wild frontier. A few of the leading comic books offered some insight to the thinking of people in the scientific world.

Newspapers, magazines, and radios were not a part of our world during the days when we were growing up. Our introduction to the radio was by a neighbor who had rigged up a power system with an automobile battery, and occasionally invited us in for an evening's entertainment, but the reception of the audio was very poor, often accompanied with so much static that one had difficulty understanding the messages or enjoying the music.

America was stuck in both the economic and social doldrums of the day. The Depression was very difficult to overcome, and the threat of war in Europe was making life uneasy for the general population. America needed something positive to uplift her spirits, something like a national hero.

The renowned champion of the heavyweight division of the boxing world was a native of Germany who was desirous of defending his world title, and he scheduled a return match with America's foremost heavyweight representative, whom he had beaten in a previous bout. Many in America became obsessed with this second fight, mostly because the champion was a German, and Germany was Europe's number one enemy during this period. On the evening of the scheduled rematch, those who owned radios, along with invited neighbors, were glued to them to listen to the fight of the century, in hope that the American would redeem himself from the previous defeat. The fight was over before the people were settled for the festivities, but the outcome enlightened our spirits because we had a national hero at the expense of the German fighter.

In the land of Appalachia, stringed instruments were very popular, accompanied with lyrics depicting themes of broken hearts between forlorn lovers, and the comforts and support of family life. This style of music was born as hillbilly and passed through a stage called bluegrass, and today is recognized as country and western, and pop. This Appalachian culture eventually found a home in Nashville, Tennessee, supported by a powerful radio station that broadcasted lively programs each Saturday night and could be heard throughout the eastern part of the country. Those who owned radios and listened to this style of music were faithful to tune in on Saturday nights to be entertained when the famous country stars from Nashville brought the countryside to life by singing and playing their stringed instruments.

Those leading stars were instrumental in building this music industry into an identifying culture that had far-reaching changes on rural society. Young and old alike took an interest in playing the guitar, fiddle, and banjo. Local bands and singing artists performed at social functions, including nightclubs and square-dancing festivities. The older members of our family became interested in this style of music, and after acquiring guitars they attempted to become proficient and to some degree practiced their musical skills well into adulthood.

A local boy who lived on Duck Run, a small rural community just a few miles toward the south from our surroundings, began singing and playing his guitar at various social functions and apparently had unusual talent in the field of entertainment. It was told that he was dating a local girl, and when he decided to try his hand in California, she refused to go with him. Not too long after his arrival in California, he formed a band and became a favorite in western movies. In a short time, he became a national celebrity, and was the talk of our town. Local fans who followed western culture seldom missed one of his movies, and when they were advertized as coming attractions, the theater enjoyed a good audience for the duration of the showing.

Picture shows were off limits for our family, as were most all outside influences—including secular books—because they were considered to be obstacles to a good moral upbringing. We were raised to believe that everything we needed to know was written in the Bible, and secular books and movies, if we indulged in them, would play a big part in ruining the fabric of our moral society. Dad was listening while one of us was singing a song with lyrics telling that a lover was lost and gone forever and promptly turned the lyric into a spiritual message, informing us that people outside the church are lost and will go to a place in the afterlife that is too horrible to describe. However, in our later teen years after we had become more independent, we found means to visit the movie houses on the quietus, though they were nearly twenty miles away, even if a great deal of effort had to be expended to get there and back.

Some of us boys would hitch hike to Portsmouth on a Saturday evening to see a double feature (western) and stay for the late, late show, which ended at a time that we should have been in bed. Following the late movie, we then waited at the bus station until the wee hours of the morning and rode the bus to Lucasville, if we had twenty cents left over. Seven miles later, arriving home at nearly daylight and exhausted, we might wonder if it was all worth it as we sneaked under the covers to catch a little sleep before we were aroused for breakfast and the chores that lay ahead. But come another good double feature—well, sometimes we just couldn't resist!

The majority of us siblings favored the environment on Camp Creek, as many of our aunts, uncles, and cousins lived in that vicinity. After Mom died in the late thirties, close ties with our relatives on the maternal side of the family had somewhat become severed, which allowed some of us to favor loafing out at Bear Creek with the kids who went to the same school. Bear Creek was much closer and most of our activities there occurred between the Girl Scout swimming pool and the Bear Creek store, a distance of less than a mile. On a warm Sunday afternoon, as many as ten to fifteen boys, and sometimes girls, could be seen wandering aimlessly up and down the Bear Creek road. At other times, we boys were likely to have been hanging out at the store, where we were entertained with stories and gossip from the older men.

One warm Sunday when everything was quiet around the store, several of us boys ambled west on the Bear Creek road to break out of the doldrums of the afternoon to stir up a little excitement. We shortly entered a graveled road where an old shanty stood among the trees, furbished with two windows, one on each side of the entrance door. Following a couple dares, the shattering of glass began to excite everyone in the group, and in just a minute or so several of the large pebbles from the road bed found a new home inside the living room and bedrooms of that old house. Destruction of property rarely goes unnoticed, and the next week the culprits were confronted with their abuses and were warned of the consequences if restitution wasn't made in short order. The two days' wages earned in cutting weeds from the river bottom cornfields made those few moments of pleasure very expensive.

The social lives of young people in the community were mostly on a hit and skip basis. Aside from church participation, most of our cultural activities were spontaneous. Group sleigh riding in the winter was a memorable event. A big bonfire near the bottom of a hill provided a warm atmosphere after a downhill run, and we sometimes enjoyed an evening of sleigh riding that often lasted until nearly midnight. The cold of the winter night didn't sting so much if one had his favorite riding on the sleigh with him!

Fifteen Kids
and
an Old Blind Horse

The elementary school rarely if ever held activities to entertain the community, as it didn't have facilities like a gymnasium for social gatherings or sports. During our high school days, the local school bus ran its regular school route in the evenings to transport students who were desirous of attending our high school basketball games. This was a fun time and our students weren't left out of the social activities of the high school. The ride home in a darkened bus with your favorite girl nestling her head on your shoulder completed another memorable day in the life of a rural teenager.

On warm summer evenings when there weren't any social activities going on, like church doings, or when things were quiet at the local store, several of us boys would congregate near the steps of the township house, or anywhere in the middle of the Bear Creek road, and entertain ourselves with unsavory jokes and community gossip that shouldn't have been repeated.

One family in the community, having four young ladies who liked to square dance, invited some of us lads to their home on Saturday nights where we enjoyed lively hoe-downs. The furniture in the large living room would be set along the walls, records with music and square dance calls were put on the "talking machine," and we were in for a lively evening of square dancing and entertainment. Incidentally, those girls were very good singers, and occasionally they were invited to sing for the local radio station. Their mother always had a pie in the cupboard for a treat before we ventured out in the cold winter night.

Upon arrival at their home, when the weather was very cold, the car's radiator, suffering from needing antifreeze, had to be drained to prevent freezing. After leaving the party, rather than refill the radiator and drain it again, we ran the car hard for a short distance to get up speed and turned off the ignition before the engine became overheated, and coasted as far as we could. It took a little longer to get home using this method, but we didn't have to be out in the cold to winterize the car in the middle of the night.

Regional areas of the country have many peculiarities indigenous to their culture. In many communities, especially among the rural areas, when couples committed themselves to a lifetime of matrimony, relatives and friends would decide that it was time to officially welcome them into the community as a married family. While most young couples expected and prepared for such social events, they just didn't know when it was going to happen. It was a custom for most people to retire shortly after dark, especially newlyweds, so the early night hours were deemed to be the appropriate time to entertain them, as it was most likely that both the bride and groom would be at home, and in bed! The setting was complete to have a belling for the newlyweds!

The belling party would congregate near the home of the newlyweds and interrupt the tranquillity of the evening by singing love songs, ringing bells, firing shotguns, and rattling the front door to rouse the couple from their "slumber." Following a short interlude to compose themselves, the newlyweds emerged in the living quarters, pretending they had been awakened from a deep sleep, and invite the party into their home and treat them with candy and cigars. Following a period of congratulations and social exchanges, the belling party would leave and the newlywed, having survived the post-matrimonial initiation festivities, would have no reason to anticipate further interruptions.

If one member of the newlyweds was from a slightly different culture that was not accustomed to such social mores, the activities of the belling party may be taken as an affront, and the native member would have some explaining to do.

Sometimes there would be a cat and mouse game between the belling party and the newlyweds. The newlyweds may frown at such intrusions, and the custom was that if either of the newlyweds, generally the groom, was not at home, the celebration would be called off and planned, unannounced, for a future date. This social sparring was mostly for bragging rights, as was the custom, and everyone assumed all newlyweds would be belled...in due time. The groom countered with a silent challenge: “catch me if you can!” Eventually, whether or not the belling celebration was successful, both parties would cheerfully call a truce.

It was imperative to have a calendar in rural homes to keep us informed concerning the weather, the phases of the moon, and other solar activities, along with the days and months of the year. Most calendars of that day were printed on large sheets of thin paper and were sponsored by funeral homes and other retail outlets. They not only listed the current year, month, and day, but included such bits of information as the time of the day's sunrise and sunset, the phases of the moon, the Zodiac clock, and a small emblem that indicated the day's weather forecast, a year in advance!

The Zodiac clock represented twelve astrological divisions, one for each month, but each division was further broken down with signs that suggested the proper day for planting various garden seeds. Planting a particular seed one day before or after the proper sign would have considerable bearing on the success of the crop. Most older folk, especially small farmers and gardeners, relied heavily on this information to ensure they would plant their crops on the proper date and get the best yield.

Old timers advised that vegetables that bore fruit on the stem should not be planted in the sign of the "posies," as it was believed the plants would bloom profusely without producing a good quality or quantity of fruit! Just one day in planting error could lead to a severe reduction in harvest. Potatoes must be planted following the first full moon after the spring equinox. When planted properly, it was believed this root crop would grow deeper and produce more abundantly. Good Friday was the best day for planting potatoes!

Our grandma believed in the sign of the Zodiac and followed the planting directions religiously. Grandchildren who stayed overnight at her house were reminded that they must return as soon as their chores were finished and help her prepare the ground for planting a certain vegetable that day. The older folks believed that many of their ailments could be alleviated if one prescribed or applied the proper remedy at the right time of the Zodiac.

We didn't always rely on the accuracy of the calendar and discovered that reading certain weather signs would give a more reliable picture of the weather pattern in the short term than did the calendar. While there were many natural weather signs, not all could be relied on to plan for outside work, but a few were quite popular, and farmers and outdoors men regularly observed the heavenly atmosphere to determine short-term forecasts. Red clouds in the evening were fairly reliable forecast for a good working day tomorrow! Red clouds in the morning would likely give the farmer a free day from the fields, as it would probably rain. If it rained early in the morning, unless it was a general soaking, the afternoon would likely be dry. These observations weren't accurate all the time, but in general, they were reasonably reliable. Such was the weather forecast before the science of the electronic communications age.

Finally, those old calendars highlighted the major holidays of the season. Many of the holidays were not celebrated to any degree by our family, and we were not ones to show off by celebrating them with extravagance. New Year's celebrations were not in vogue, and we reflected very little on other late winter and spring holidays, excepting Valentine's Day. While not officially celebrated as one of the important national holidays, we created our valentines and the teachers dismissed class for a short period before going home for us to exchange valentines with our favorites. Valentine's Day became a big hit with schoolchildren, as well as older lovers!

Our rural churches didn't elaborate on the period of Lent, Good Friday, and Easter, until these holidays were made popular by movies and other commercial advertising. Memorial Day was rarely observed except that it marked the end of the school year and ushered in the beginning of summer.

The first real holiday of the year that we enjoyed was the Fourth of July, which offered a break from the long hot summer. A few families from Portsmouth weekended at their cabins along the Scioto River, and occasionally we stationed ourselves along the canal road near the cabin area to watch their annual fireworks display. The Fourth also marked the date when the little roosters that we had cared for all spring were deemed to be large enough for fryers, and it was a custom to eat fried chicken on that holiday. It was hoped that we didn't have a company of aunts and uncles, as small children were the last to be seated at the dinner table and all the good pieces of the chicken would have been eaten by the time there was room at the table for us. It seemed that they lingered too long at the table while talking about politics and social conditions, without considering that we children were more desirous of relieving our hunger than listening to their talking!

Other notable holidays were Halloween, as mentioned beforehand, Thanksgiving, and Christmas. Thanksgiving, one of the more important holidays of our era, was a time enjoyed at family gatherings, but not of the scale of modern times.

Most churches entertained the community with an annual Christmas program, and several evenings in the month of December were set aside for practice. Participation in the Christmas program at the local church was a time for making connections with other boys and girls in the community, and many of us desired to be annual participants for the social benefits. The program would be presented on the night before Christmas, and was always a success as parents flocked to the church to watch their children in the performance.

Very few families or churches put up decorations for the holidays, as the church hierarchy didn't believe decorations or a Christmas tree should play a part in the annual holiday celebration. The church long ago determined that Christmas decorations were of pagan origin and it would not be acceptable to violate the mores and teachings of the church, as these directives were handed down from the heads of the denominations, who were the authorities in determining what was right and wrong for our church society.

Our family celebrated Christmas at home with Dad retrieving a sack from a hiding place in the house after the morning chores had been completed. The sack generally contained an orange or an apple apiece, and occasionally a pair of socks or a small inexpensive toy of some kind. Within a few minutes the celebration was over, and we treated the rest of the day as just another day and went on with our daily routine.

We lived in what may be called a homogeneous setting in relation to our relatives, as most families of kin lived within a radius of three or four miles and could offer support to each other. We thought nothing of walking that far to see our maternal grandmother without being invited. (We often took a shortcut through a wooded valley referred to as Hungry Hollow, a distance of about two miles where Grandma lived on Camp Creek.) An extra plate would be set on the table at mealtime and we felt most welcome. During the evenings, we younger ones would sit on the floor and listen to all sorts of stories being told by aunts and uncles, always revealing that their formidable years were much more difficult when they were growing up as compared to the present. If we planned to stay the night, a pallet would be made on the floor.

Grandma and our uncles were having the same economic difficulty, as was the rest of the population. If we visited her when her sons were present, it seemed to us younger ones that their serious talks were always secretive and in low tones. We later learned their privacy was to prevent us from being exposed to information concerning their illicit activities that might cause them serious trouble with law enforcement officers, as some had resorted to making and selling moonshine to provide money for their family's needs. It has been said that our uncles could distill a batch of spirits "as good as could be run off."

Though some of our relatives were advocates of this easy money, and while Dad never openly criticized their activities, we knew there were strained relations among members of the clan, and we children were discouraged from spending too much time at their homes. Distillers naturally helped themselves to their product, and after a long period of indulging their attitudes could be measured against the amount of spirits they consumed.

There was no day-to-day communication among our families, and aunts and cousins, without invitation or warning, might become weekend visitors. Our parents, who were already struggling to provide a meager existence for their own brood, no doubt found additional mouths more of a burden than a blessing, but they were always welcome and we seemed to manage. To us younger children company was great, and we enjoyed playing with someone other than members of our own family.

When we swapped an item of clothing, even though it may have been well worn, to us it was like getting something new. Hand-me-down pieces were most appreciated. While Mom and Dad struggled to find the essential necessities to provide for a weekend visit, we children saw those visits through different eyes, and their company caused us to become quite close and we shared a lot in common.

An aunt on Dad's side, from Lucasville, came to the hill and visited Grandma every few weeks, mostly on Sunday, and would plan to stay with her the biggest part of the day. When Grandma entertained company, we children weren't permitted to go to her house until the dinner hour was over, as dinner was for company only, and since we lived so close our family was never referred to as company, so members of our immediate family were seldom if ever invited to dinner with Grandma. When our aunt visited Grandma, her husband visited his relatives in the nearby Camp Creek community and seldom made the mile walk to the top of the hill with his wife and children.

When our uncle did accompany them, the men would sit in the living room on Sunday afternoons and reminisce about religion and world conditions, such as crime, politics, the punishment of the nether world, or the war that Germany was waging in Europe. These sessions were spiced with graphic language and frequently included a few derogatory remarks about people of different races and especially those whose religious values were not as righteous as ours. Many times those conversations contained ideas that young people shouldn't hear.

Dad was never fond of engaging in a conversation with detrimental remarks about other people, but this kind of talk seemed to surface and become the topic of the day. We children could only sit and listen, as youngsters weren't permitted to speak unless they were asked to do so, which was very seldom, as the adults believed children were too immature to have anything to contribute to the conversation.

It was a custom that when company prepared to end their visitation, we children would walk down the road with them until we reached the top of the hill, where the road, after meandering a short distance through a wooded area, began a steep descent toward the river valley below. One afternoon the conversation was unusually graphic about the war in Europe, filling our little minds with fear and uncertainty. When the visitation concluded, we children were accompanying our guests as they were leaving, and a couple of us ran ahead of the pack, and to our bewilderment this huge figure jumped out of the woods in front of us emitting horrific screams, causing flashbacks of those gruesome images we had been exposed to just a few minutes earlier. Well, our little feet did an about-face and we raced back to the safety of the company to whom we were about to say farewell. We were taught to honor grown-up people by addressing them with respect, but honoring that uncle became very difficult after scaring us as he did. He wasn't a favorite person until we had grown up enough to appreciate the humor of such incidents!

Dad's progenitors lived on the Sedan area, located about four miles toward the western section of Morgan

Township, and we weren't well-acquainted with them as we hardly visited each other. Their overall achievements in life were greater than ours, which no doubt caused the parties to keep their distances. Additionally, it was much farther to walk to their farm, making access to them more laborious, and somehow we just didn't feel comfortable showing up without an invitation. Dad seldom said much, but we learned that silence has a way of telling its own story.

There was very little enforcement of the laws concerning the behavior of minors who desired to indulge in worldly vices—practiced and enjoyed by adults—before reaching the age of responsibility. Few rural store owners questioned the purchasing of tobacco products by minors and it was easy to have an adult purchase alcoholic beverages, although we seldom had the financial means to indulge in this vice.

A neighbor who worked in Portsmouth with whom we often hitched a ride home would oblige in filling our request if we desired some spirits for the weekend. One Saturday evening, two of us lads, probably sixteen at that time, had a few cents left over after taking in the town and watching the matinee of a favorite western. Having walked to the street corner where the neighbor was to drive by on his way home, and after he had stopped to give us a ride, we "persuaded" him to stop at the wine store and purchase a pint of wine for our weekend entertainment. That wine was very cheap— most likely rotgut that was consumed by winos—and we were a sorry mess come Sunday morning. Wine has never been a favorite beverage to this day, and to him a gratitude of thanks for that weekend encounter!

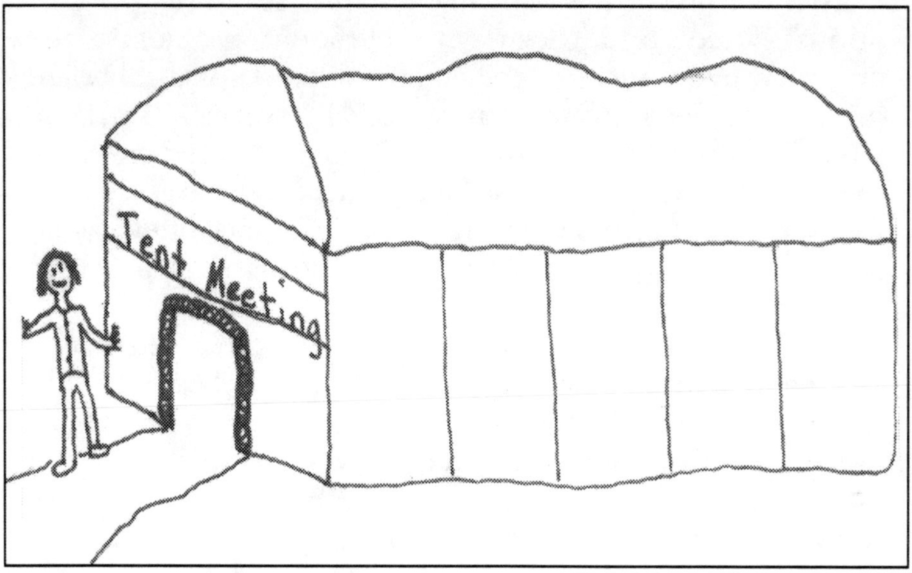

12. Going to Church

The older generations of our family believed that religion was the primary reason for living. Attendance at religious services was not only of paramount importance, but a sacred duty; therefore, the church was the most important cultural center in the neighborhood. To survive, the church needed as many members as it could get, but it had to offer a return to entice the flock to come in. As members of the church, both the poor and the more well-to-do were somewhat equals, at least in religious matters and during the worship services. A person having a good grasp of his faith always stood out among the congregation, regardless of his economic and social standings.

To those on the low rung of economic standing, the sick and afflicted, and those with personal problems, the church offered hope. To the poor, it offered spiritual relief, if just for a few minutes during worship service. To those who seemingly had no future, the church offered gracious rewards in the afterlife. Their faith in these rewards relieved them temporarily from the drudgery of everyday life, poverty, and hard work, with the hope of a future eternal life.

Parents and the children in our family, dressed in our best each Sunday morning, climbed into the bed of the old wagon and off to church we'd go, sometimes up to three or four miles away. One can imagine what time it was and how hungry we were by the time we had been warned of the world's evils before making the return journey home. While attendance during our very early years was compulsory, participation later on was at each individual's discretion and church attendance became more or less a social activity, especially for the younger set. Some of us participated in various seasonal performances at the church, which allowed interaction with other youth in the area.

Most rural churches held Sunday evening meetings and it was a staging area for teenagers to hang out, although most of us seldom went inside the church. At times, there were nearly as many young people in the church parking lot as there were adults in the Sunday services, especially in the evenings. The church was definitely the social center of rural areas during this period.

The social connections following church, especially those evening sessions, were periods of time when an occasional engagement between a boy and a girl might occur. It was a pleasure for a young lad to pair up with his favorite and walk her home on a dark night...to protect her from the creatures of the wilds! Naturally, those minutes of bliss would carry over to the next day at school, but who wants to think about that now? Well! Many of us attended church doings for the social contacts rather than trying to improve on our morals and behavior.

The more memorable religious meetings, outside the mainlined church, occurred almost yearly in our community. It was the coming of the tent meeting evangelist. This tent meeting evangelist was a professional, and he earned his livelihood by going to various communities within a twenty-five-mile radius or so and presiding over tent meetings throughout the warm months of the year. In the colder winter months, he would "borrow" the township hall or any public building that was available, perhaps a local church sympathetic to his cause, and hold the meetings on the inside.

Periodically, he would arrive with a large tent, and with the assistance of the local people erect it in an open space large enough to accommodate the traffic. It didn't take much room as most people in the near vicinity walked to the meeting each night, and very little space was required for parking automobiles. After the furniture was carried in, including a platform to be stationed at the front of the tent that was large enough to accommodate five or six chairs for visiting evangelists, the tent would be ready for the evening services and the welcome signal would go out for all to come and join in the festivities.

The first couple of meetings would be somewhat mundane, with the evangelist warming up to the people and the people warming up to the evangelist. About the third night, one could observe a change that would set the tone for the next three or four weeks, maybe more. The songs became more lively when a few amens, glories, and hallelujahs began to permeate the atmosphere, and shortly the Holy Ghost would send a season of inspiration upon the worshipers in the tent meeting. Long-winded testimonies, a few praises about the Lord's work and what the Lord and done for various individuals, more singing, and passing the collection...er, offering plate were followed with a long prayer session for the purpose of determining which one of the visiting preachers was going to have the honor of bringing the evening message. It was a customary procedure for the platform guests to "lay hands" on the evening speaker, anointing him with the power of the Holy Ghost, before he was to bring the evening message—and it's getting well into an hour already.

Nightly, the evangelists wove into their litany the perils of evil living and the cardinal sins of our time. They included drinking, card-playing, gambling, attending movies—these were the works of the devil, along with cursing, using tobacco, and occasionally adultery, which seldom if ever occurred in our rural setting...at least no one talked much about that subject. These evils were illustrated nightly by combining them with long-winded sermons detailing the disobedience of Jonah who was swallowed by the whale, or Elijah running away from God, and Noah getting drunk and backsliding. Their messages were always spiced with the theme of a judgment with a burning fire and damnation to follow, a litany that could make the hair on the back of one's neck prickle.

We were reminded every night that sinners would burn in hades for millions of years with O' Satan himself, and we were warned not to get in step with the old devil as it gets awfully hot where he is going! If the evangelistic meetings were held during the winter in the township hall, it didn't matter if the fire in the heating stove went out or not, we were all fanning ourselves to keep cool anyway. It has been said that more people have been scared out of flames of fire than those who went to the good place because they loved someone!

In most of the socially minded mainlined churches, the road to church membership, or salvation, started at a very early age. In infancy, parents would bring their newborn babes to church to be baptized, dedicated, and consecrated. The infant's parents would take vows to bring their child up in a Christian-like atmosphere until the time they reached the age of accountability. (Following this public showing of ecclesiastical interest, many would never darken the church doors again, unless a wedding or a funeral commanded their attendance). When a lull of about twelve years had passed, and the babes were deemed to have reached the age to know right from wrong—some sects believed this age to be as low as eight while others would assign the high limit of about fourteen—children were invited to attend a series of ecclesiastical classes during the winter months, and those who became prospective initiates would be admitted to full church membership during the worship hour on Easter Sunday morning when the church had its largest assemblage of the year. After the minister had performed the rituals of consecration, the church saints would gather around the initiates and welcome them into the fold, and the initiates became full-fledged members of the church.

This easy way to salvation is not accepted by the more conservative groups who maintain that infants and young children should not be baptized as they are not mentally developed enough to determine the proper morality of a community and to assume the privileges and responsibilities that are enjoyed with church membership. Initiation must wait until they are in their teens or twenties, or even older, to enjoy the honor and entitlement of their elders. The tent meetings provided a quick stepping stone in this process as it enjoyed a healthy exposure of people for the next few weeks and offered all that the more conservative fold desired. The tent meetings were more exciting than the mainlined church and garnered followers that the regular church could not entice.

When a new revival began, it didn't take long for some of last year's backsliders to announce that they had drifted back into sinful living, enslaved by the sins of the wicked world, since the last tent meeting, and desired to amend their ways to escape the horrors of damnation so eloquently characterized by the evangelist! These backsliders, feeling guilty because they had been told that they were weak and had strayed from their faith since the last tent meeting, and, after being reminded of the vows they had taken, were desirous of returning to the good graces of the evangelists and the Christian community.

About the fourth night, after those wayward few had become saved again, the shouting, amens, glories, and hallelujahs began to permeate the atmosphere of the tent. Joining with this spiritual crescendo, some of the newly revived converts would likely go into a frenzy. The aisles would become a circus-like scene by those who had renounced their wicked ways and were now back on the road to glory. Some held a white cloth above their heads as a sign that they had repented and to announce to everyone that they were, again, a new "born again" person. Experienced attendees quickly learned not to sit in a chair adjacent to the aisle, for by the time the shouting and amens were over, they would have been hugged and kissed a dozen times and their shirt sleeves would be wet from wiping those happy tears from their faces.

Following the lengthy sermon by the anointed guest evangelist, supported by the platform guests with a bevy of amens and praises to agree that the truth was being heard from the anointed one, the leading evangelist would call for hymns of spiritual persuasion that reminded us of our unworthiness and sinful ways, while enticing those who were feeling guilty to raise their hands for prayer, and by doing so agree with the assessment of the evangelist that they were nefarious persons as portrayed in the evening sermon. Those who responded by asking for prayer—it was suggested that we all needed it—would be considered to be under conviction and were the first to get attention from the remaining platform guests, who were already in the aisles beckoning one and all to respond to the invitation, while the altar call was being extended. Woe to those sitting along the aisle, especially if they were alone, as they would be easy targets for the evangelists whose duty was to compel those who were out of the fold to go to the altar and repent.

Meanwhile, between the numerous hymns, the tent evangelist would admonish the Holy Ghost to bring a greater conviction upon all transgressors who were present. It was believed that persons could not be received by the Almighty, unless they had been "under conviction" long enough to be thoroughly repugnant of their past sins, and have come to the station of their spirituality where they felt free to renounce and publically confess their evil past. In his appeal, the evangelist reminded us that anyone who had never made a confession of faith was living under the power of the evil one! Many penitents were under conviction for days before they could muster enough courage to come forth and openly lay their guilt before all who were in attendance.

All youth attending the meetings were approached numerous times to renounce their sinful way of life before they became calloused like the old foxes whose hearts were hardened with pride and had become too arrogant to submit. We youth soon learned there was security in numbers, and would congregate in the middle of the pews, or maybe exit to the rear of the tent to escape their appeal, making it more difficult to be accessed.

Sinners in acute despair, those who had experienced emotional or financial setbacks, would be the first to respond to the mental pressure exerted by songs and the beckoning of learned evangelists who were surely in direct contact with God, which, in all, makes one feel guilty and alone. When penitents could no longer resist the evangelist's pressures, and after being reminded that rejection enhanced the chance of going to their doom if they should die before the next scheduled meeting, they answered the call by going to the altar to make their peace with God...yet hardly anyone was ever told just how to get in contact with God except to "pray through." Apparently, revealing such ecclesiastical secrets to the common sinner would diminish the importance of the heavenly connection between God and the evangelists!

Now before they could be redeemed of their sins, prospective initiates must have been under conviction for many days to show the true sincerity of their unworthiness. To illustrate their sincerity, they must confess all their sins to the congregation, along with their most private deeds and sinister thoughts. Without full confessions, they could not be accepted by The Almighty. One can imagine how embarrassing all of this might be, or the consequences open confessions might cause family members or other innocent individuals.

When penitents openly reveal their inner souls to the community, especially if one had occasionally slipped through the back door to visit his paramour after the man of the house had gone off to work for the day...well, unpleasant consequences might occur. Most teenagers, like adults, were faced with hard decisions before confessing those sensuous moments they had enjoyed in a clandestine setting with a favorite suitor that had nurtured exquisite seasons of delight and ecstasy. Seldom did one wish to confess to the church community that card playing, drinking, gambling, and going to an occasional movie were enjoyable.

Those who responded would simply kneel at the altar and attempt to find relief from the horrible images of the nether world by praying, crying, or just hoping something would happen to relieve them of their guilt. Seldom did one get saved the first night, as the evangelist's success was to get as many sinners to the altar each night as possible. This gathering at the altar each night was a true indication that the Holy Ghost was working in the services and surely the Almighty was truly in our very midst. Verse after verse from hymns of persuasion were sung to compel the more penitent minded and to break the core of the hard-hearted.

A long session at the altar made the night short for those who had to rise early for work, and when many in the audience began to get restless, the evangelist would finally instruct the anguished souls at the altar to rise and be prepared to come back the next night to finish praying through.

After being compelled to visit the altar for three or four nights, maybe more, the repentant, being physically and emotionally drained, would rise with tears streaming from his cheeks and a smile that testified to a changed soul. Those who repented would offer an amen or two and a praise the Lord to the congregation and the platform guests. Most likely, relief came by just getting up and deciding he was not going to suffer through another night at the altar!

Now another newly saved soul is added to the congregation. Well, not yet. Being saved is just the first step in the transformation of one in the conservative salvation movement. The new saints must go on to maturity! The next stage in on the way to glory in the process of setting one apart from the world is called sanctification or holiness. Another term used to describe this stage is called perfection and is achieved by "the anointing of the Holy Ghost." Those who have been acknowledged to reach the state of holiness are very close to the throne of God, and are revered by their peers throughout the congregation. But this holiness doesn't come any easier than the first step to salvation. It requires ardent prayers and many petitions to the Holy Ghost, along with support from the evangelist and other church dignitaries. Reaching perfection is the ultimate goal in the spiritual process, and this stage of salvation is not to be taken lightly.

Having acquired perfection, there is still one more step to take before a convert is completely acceptable to enter into the pearly gates. Baptism. This may take place either before, during or after the seeking of perfection. Most generally, one must be baptized in the pure water of a running creek to wash away any sin that may not have surfaced when the penitent confessed, while saints on the shore were singing songs that offered courage to the initiates as they were being led into the water. If the profession of faith was consummated during the winter months, it was acceptable to be baptized, even if the ice had to be broken. The evangelist assured the initiate that he has never known a person to become ill from being baptized in ice cold water.

A poignant and tragic event occurred in our community when one of the tent-meeting revivals was in progress. A young man of the world who lived in the immediate area was in attendance one night after he had become somewhat inebriated. Subsequently, he was approached by one of the evangelists and encouraged to change his way of living, but didn't accept the challenge, and that following weekend or so was killed by a family member as he was entering his home. It was said that he was under the influence and with an axe in hand, after slashing partially through the upstairs bedroom door, was shot and killed in self-defense, supposedly by his wife.

This tragedy fueled an argument about the concept of judgment and the punishment of the wicked in the fire of eternal torment, motivated by the sermons we had been hearing in the tent meeting. A stirring discussion ensued concerning the eternal assignment of that young man's soul since he had apparently died in the state of transgression. The evangelist had charged each and every evening that persons who lived villainous lives and died in iniquity went immediately to the place we all wanted to avoid. For some reason, after a few evenings of holy inspiration, no one seemed to mourn for that lost soul, though we were all convinced that he had been assigned to this awesome and wretched state of perpetual agony. Oh well, out of sight, out of mind!

For us serious-minded male teenagers, our eyes were generally focused toward the seats where the more fair sex sat, and after approach were acknowledged with a return smile or a rosy blush, we knew we were in the clover and there would be more to this tent meeting than amens and hallelujahs. Following the evening services, with mutual desires, our relationships were extended as long as possible, with the moonbeams dancing in her eyes while her embraces excited the youthful passion of her escort, but eventually the evening's flirtation would end with a passionate farewell just before she glided up the pathway and vanished through the front door. Our minds were already engrossed with the anticipation of the pleasures of tomorrow night!

Well, these meetings would go on for several weeks, much to the delight of some of us younger sinners. After several weeks of continuous revival, a special service was announced to proclaim the crowning achievement of sanctification and humility. There was gonna be a foot washing. When the announced date arrived, the tent meeting evangelist would fetch a pan of water and towel—no soap—kneel before the subordinate servants on the podium, remove their shoes and socks, and perform the ritual of washing their feet. Shortly, they would be washing each other's feet amid the chorus of amens, glories, and hallelujahs, while the pianist softly played hymns to reflect the setting. No one explained why the people in the audience were unworthy of having their feet washed. After all, they had been paying for something every night!

By the time of the foot washing celebration, several new initiates had been brought into the fold, along with most of the backsliders who were saved during the previous tent meeting. The evangelists had given up on the stiff-necked persons as they were assumed to be unreachable, and therefore relegating themselves to a life of misery. In spite of the failure to convert everyone in the community, the meetings were deemed successful.

Eventually, all good things must come to an end, and the tent meeting evangelist would announce that this would be the last week of meetings, as the Holy Ghost had done all it could in the community. We teenagers knew there was another reason. At the beginning, when financial support was requested, the collections contained a few pieces of paper, but the time came when the evangelist heard too much clinking as the metal plates were being passed. When this behavior became a nightly ritual, an announcement was soon forthcoming that arrangements were being made for the evangelist to find newer pastures. However, we were assured that the community would be ripe for another visit next year. The same announcement revealed the location for the next series of meetings, starting next week, and we were all invited.

On the appointed day of departure, with the help of the supporting stalwarts and some of the new converts, the furniture was packed, the tent torn down, and, as the truck was being driven to the new destination, all of us were reminded that another ecclesiastical year had been one to remember. For some of us, going to the tent meetings wasn't over for the year. One of the community preachers portrayed himself as an official dignitary of the church by posing as a man of the cloth. In church circles he was akin to a man without a country, as he never assumed direct responsibility for a community parish, nor did he practice to any degree his moral virtues among the neighbors. He often traveled to the surrounding tent meetings and churches where revivals were held, and did encourage some of us youngsters to go to church with him, especially the nights when he was invited to deliver the sermon. He picked up several boys and girls on the route to the church, to the delight of us youngsters. We rode in the back of his farm truck that had a canvas tied over the top and fastened to the side rails to afford us protection from wind and any inclement weather that might occur. This arrangement was fitting for us older teens and we enjoyed some memorable times under that old canvass. While we looked forward to going to these meetings, we knew he was using us to help fill empty seats in an effort to make a personal impression, as he liked to announce to the congregation the number of people he had brought to church that evening.

While our community in general wasn't any more religious than other neighborhood, toleration was an anathema by many white Protestant church members, as well as most of the local population. Jews, people of another color or race, Catholics, and competing Protestants who may have a different religious view than we were frowned upon.

A family in our own community, living just a few hundred feet from a nearby church and the usual site of the tent meetings, believed it was evil to salute, pay homage to or bow down to false images, such as flags or sacred symbols that represent either secular or religious allegiance. Though they belonged to another congregation and were free to worship as they pleased, the good souls in our community refused to accept them as self respected citizens, but did tolerate their living amongst us, barely. However, an abnormal spirit of patriotism surfaced when the war started during the early forties, and anyone who appeared to be against the war effort was scorned by the community.

Adults of their persuasion believed war to be immoral and refused to join the armed forces and participate openly in uniform. To add insult to injury, their children refused to salute the American flag with the other students in school. This anti-American behavior caused them to be labeled as unpatriotic and un-Christian by our good people. We children at school chimed in with a righteous indignation that inflicted condemnation upon those children who were as innocent and ignorant of the accusations as we were.

Dad, being recognized as an authority and interpreter of the Protestant faith, or maybe he was just a conscientious proselyte, was occasionally approached by the more knowledgeable devotees of other faiths who desired to make him realize the error of his way. We remembered one such encounter when a member of a religious body having opposing beliefs and Dad sat on Grandma's porch one Sunday afternoon and debated their differences in theology, with both debaters failing to crack the armor of the faith of the other. After listening to them for a season of debating using such terms as born again, second blessing, and sanctification, one was most anxious to slip away and enjoy the beauty of nature, which was much easier to appreciate.

There were many in the area who seldom if ever darkened the door of the church or entered those tent meetings, but the church did have a lasting effect on the people as a whole. Regardless of one's persuasion, the religious influence was quite effective in determining the mores, beliefs, and morality of the people. Whether individuals went to church or not, their lives were affected by the code of conduct that the community adopted from the teachings of the church.

13. Religious values

Southern Ohio is in a geographical area that people of faith refer to as the Bible belt. Although there were some industrial facilities that provided a few good jobs, the area as a whole could be referred to as Appalachia, and the mean income per family was by no means average to that of the more northern regions in Ohio.

The general standard of living, because of chronic depression and family reversals, seemed to have caused a fair number of citizens to turn to God and rely upon Him for their strength. Faith was important when making decisions, and morality became the gold standard of righteousness.

Regardless of their economic plight, people of faith held

themselves in high esteem, believing that they had received a mandate from God to set an example for the community's moral conduct. They established themselves as the spiritual leaders of society and were obligated to inaugurate a high standard of morality for all citizens to observe. Consequently, unwritten rules of morality became the mores of the community, to be observed by all residents, hopefully.

Their unwritten code of ethics led to many yeas and nays in respectable goings-on. Those who did not present themselves for the two-hour worship period on Sunday and attend other scheduled prayer and study activities were considered to be on the cutting edge of the mercy of God and were targets for redemptive action. While these apostates were referred to as good neighbors and socially upright and responsible citizens, they just didn't have the true love of God and mankind that sets them apart from the members of the kingdom.

Working on the Sabbath was very likely to reap moral and mortal consequences, thus, very little activity transpired in the community in the way of physical production. It was a sin to work on Sunday, and those who did would quickly be inflicted by the wrath of God. Bad luck was certainly the result of those who transgressed the spirit of the Lord's day. This bad luck extended to crop failure, sickness, loss of domestic animals, or any other setback the offender might suffer.

One local farmer, somewhat disinclined to observe the thinking of the moralists, constantly worked in his fields on the Sabbath. All of us knew that someday he would surely go to the dark and torturous nether world, as he continued to reject the high road to righteous living, and everyone knew it was just a matter of time. Well, we finally got proof that God really did inflict the disobedient. While working in the fields, he was come upon by a hard rainstorm, got soaking wet, and before he could get dried out was afflicted with a bad cold or some other illness and died within a few days. This was further proof that our moral status was being monitored, not only by the righteous in the community, but by God Himself!

However, the local barber, a stalwart farmer in the neighborhood who habitually cut hair on Sunday, escaped the moral wrath of the church, and lived well into the tenth decade of life. He generally opened his barbershop just after the church bell rang and finished his barbering before noon, escaping the watchful eyes of those who were returning from church. These Sunday mornings were memorable ones for those of us who congregated on his front porch, telling jokes, swapping tales that had been circulating in the community, smoking or chewing a little, and just hanging out. Once in a while we would get a ten-cent hair cut. While these activities were looked upon with moral disdain, these Sunday mornings were relished and enjoyed by those of us who were not yet indoctrinated by the high moral standards that might come upon us later in life. Some of us never did get it!

Though one should never broach the subject of having a mercantile enterprise open for business on the Sabbath, our local storekeeper escaped much of the criticism when he opened his store on Sunday afternoons, as he sold gasoline and other needed staples that our good citizens had neglected to stock up on before the weekend rolled around. Sometimes necessity became an overriding influence, and in certain instances morality would be put on the back burner by those who promoted it most when they desired to go to the store for a needed item.

The officials at the Girl Scout camp had a full schedule of activities on Sunday, and the camp was referred to by the locals as a beehive of immorality. Children should be with their families and attend church meetings on Sunday instead of frolicking the hills, playing games, and swimming in, well, "almost nude" conditions! While this was a private camp, it was well known that operations of this nature would have extreme moral consequences on the future lives of those young girls.

There were gray activities in the neighborhood that might be tolerated and even overlooked, but having a nudist ranch nearby pressed the issue too far, even for many of the less righteous. The founding mothers frequently talked and gossiped of the evil that these city folk practiced behind those fences, exercising their right to frolic near our turf without any modesty whatsoever. We youngsters were not a little apprehensive about all this talk, and our appetite for the unknown was stimulated when we were warned of the evil activities that were going on up there.

Curiosity finally got the best of us and the desire to see some of those nudist people slinking between the pine trees and acting in such immoral ways were too much for us teenagers to ignore. All of this talk challenged some of us lads to explore the outer boundaries of the ranch to determine if the old folk were really telling it like it was, or if some tall tales were just floating about the community. As we boldly advanced near the front part of the ranch—several times, and always on the alert if a fast getaway became imminent—we failed to find any evidence of immorality or that the wrath of God had struck anyone down who had visited the ranch. We were most put out because of our failure to discover naked people frolicking through the woods and meadows!

A small village called Coopersville was located about two miles north near the canal road from our home. It consisted of a combined post office and grocery store, and we kids were frequently assigned the job of running to the store for coal oil or other needful items. In our formidable years, we were somewhat apprehensive about going to that store by ourselves, as a morally offensive character who earned his living by bootlegging, gambling, and other unsavory vices that were offensive to the community lived along the canal road near the store, and we were constantly warned of the evils that were taking place in the house of the devil.

When we went to the store for Grandma, she always warned us to walk wide of his establishment and shun any invitation that might be forthcoming. (She felt that we needed these instructions, and though we were too young and without monetary means to indulge in his activities, they would serve us well when the time temptation would overcome us!) Relief came when he eventually relocated his enterprise on the Camp Creek road adjacent to one of the more conservative churches, much to the consternation of the good folk who had to walk wide of his establishment on their way to worship. No doubt his industry gave rise to a lot of savory topics for the local minister for his Sunday-morning sermons.

As one can imagine, the church was very influential in the area of morality, but it also influenced the ways people used their resources. Churches are in constant need of money to enhance their programs, and their continued pressure for support was considerable. The leaders were not bashful when informing the congregation about tithing—or 10 percent of all their income belonging to God—and that one cannot really be a good Christian if they deny God his rightful tithes. Offerings were gifts beyond the 10 percent, and when one reaches that level of giving, everything is right with their salvation! This pressure was a cause for many members to pledge their support to the needs of the church, even if the pledge denied their families of some of the bare necessities that made life more bearable.

It has been told by the older members of the family that our parents succumbed to an urgent appeal and scratched for a long period of time to save a few dollars for the cause, which in effect did deny the family of urgently needed household staples and clothing. Having made the pledge and finally gifting it to the church coffers, all was well and it was believed that the officials would wisely account for these funds with good stewardship, a term they always used when discussing communal funds.

In this incident, and others as well, it was discovered that the funds were applied toward personal benefits of the hierarchy at the expense and suffering of desperate families. Needless to say, future requests from our parents for special projects went unheeded, and Dad did remark that it was getting very hard to trust people anymore. No doubt, he lost his faith in tithing. To many members, however, the teachings of the church were sanctimonious, and just because there were a few rotten apples at the top, it didn't mean that the whole congregation was spoiled!

Whether these strict codes of morality and stewardship were accepted beyond the Bible believers is difficult to determine. Many offspring rejected this code of conduct, to the dismay of their parents, and although the churches survived, there appeared to be no real influx of followers.

14. War

The decade of the forties brought far-reaching changes for all people in America. The Axis powers were desirous of strangling the nations of the world with their theology and autocracy, without regard to the cost of suffering and destruction that invaded nations were to endure. The Japanese army had been invading nations in Southeast Asia for nearly a decade with the intention of controlling the entire eastern theater of humanity, under the tyrannical disguise of Bushido idealism, a warrior code ideology that prized honor above life and ranked surrender to the enemy as the lowest and most despicable behavior a Samurai soldier or nation could engage in. This indoctrination demanded that soldiers fight to the death and never surrender to the enemy.

Meanwhile, in Europe, the Nazi party in Germany implemented a grand plan of ethnic cleansing, a plan to rid that part of the world of all undesirables, including Jews, Gypsies, the disabled, or anyone whose veins did not run red with Aryan blood, being of sound body and a healthy mind.

America had been a sleeping nation for ten years or more, trying to work itself out of one of the greatest economic reversals in its history. The lack of demand for goods and services caused considerable unemployment. The war on both fronts had been in process for more than two years, but America refrained from taking up arms, even though her Allies were being overwhelmed with sudden invasions.

Our family heard the news from a neighbor who possessed one of the few radios in the community that one of our territories had been bombed by the Japanese navy. Few of us knew the location of Pearl Harbor or how it was connected with our country, but in a very short time, those two words became the battle cry of World War II, and would change the lives of all people in America. The bombing of Pearl Harbor was an event that awakened our nation and unified it as no other act in its one hundred and fifty-year history, and caused America to enter the global struggle that would last for nearly four more years.

As our armed forces were in a state of disarray, it was of paramount importance to raise and train a fighting force as quickly as possible to defend our shores and repel the enemy. Young men and women by the thousands were conscripted or enlisted in the military services. At the height of the great war, nearly seventeen million American citizens were in uniform and engaging in military operations.

In just a short period of time, the economic engines of

America's industry were up and running. Industrial plants that had been idle or that had previously produced domestic products were quickly retooled for the production of war materials, and would continue to do so for the duration. Most able-bodied men and women who were engaged in this great industrial expansion moved from the communities where they had grown up and settled in faraway industrial centers. The demand for war materials was so great that industrial plants hired thousands of sixteen- and seventeen-year-olds, and anyone who worked in such facilities could work as many hours a day as they could stand on their feet. Local farmers and other small enterprises hired teenagers to replace those who had gone to military service and the manufacturing cities.

Agricultural products were suddenly in great demand, and many young farmers received deferments from the armed services to help operate the family farm. The young and healthy men of the farm who received deferments were often looked upon as persons shirking their country's duty and were sometimes asked why they weren't on the war front with their neighboring friends, but as the war wore on and a great number of young people were losing their lives on the battlefield, persons with financial means began to find ways to keep their sons and daughters from harm's way.

Many upper-class families who lived in the cities and had sons of military age suddenly became farmers, and their sons operated the farm from the vantage point of the city. The farm became a front for a deferment, and once obtained they more or less became just overseers, as the tenants who had worked the land before the war continued to operate the farm under the new ownership. Families who had sons and daughters in the military services believed those persons had influence with the draft board and looked upon the new owners as draft dodgers. Many who were legally excused from the draft were persons classified as 4/F, being physically or mentally unable to pass the military examination.

The war began to change the mores of all America. Women by now were becoming engaged in the industrial sector, moving to the larger cities where they were employed in the production of war materials. With more money in circulation and the desire to find relief from long hours of working on the assembly line, a new culture dominated by a flourishing night life surfaced in our industrial centers.

Those of us who remained at home were reminded of the struggle our nation was engaged in when relatives and friends come home from the service on furlough. We were awed when seeing them in their smartly tailored uniforms and hearing their stories about life in the military. The stay-at-home girls especially relished these furloughs as so many of them missed the pleasures of young male companionship, and it was a delight for them to be seen in the company of a uniformed armed service member.

While the country as a whole was becoming as active as a beehive, our little family on the hill was scarcely touched and our activities in the economic world did not progress from the arcane schemes that had been employed by the last three generations.

As with all materials, there was a great need for timber products, for both paper and lumber. Our land was adjacent to a property with hundreds of acres of good standing timber, consisting of mature hardwood species. A local enterprise moved in to harvest the crop, and we enjoyed being around them as they worked in the woods. For us youngsters, this timber work was both fascinating and entertaining. Timber crews fell and trimmed the trees, and cut the trunks to desired lengths. These logs would be removed from the woods with oxen and stacked in the loading yard where they were loaded on trucks that hauled to the sawmill.

One fascinating part of the operation was the snaking or dragging the logs out of the woods. All hard labor at that time was executed by domestic animals—seldom was any mechanical machinery used. One particular teamster worked oxen to snake the logs out of the woods. Occasionally he worked two yokes of oxen at the same time! We were amused to watch him head his legions toward the log road leading into the woods, grab a tail of one of the trailing oxen, and disappear into the forest.

A grappling hook was a metal tool with a large claw that curved forward, and when pounded into the logs and hooked to a chain tethered to the yoke, a heavy wooden beam was placed over the necks of each oxen that harnessed them together, and the logs were ready to be dragged from the forest to the loading yard. Oxen were somewhat slow, but a well-trained yoke was safe and reliable when working in the woods, and was also quite efficient.

The timber crew set up camp near the area where they were harvesting the trees, and lived in the woods during the work week. Since oxen were slow-moving beasts, the timber men sheltered them among the trees during weeknights, rather than removing them from the woods. It was much easier to haul water and grain to the campsite than truck the animals back and forth each day.

The evening hours presented a time for telling stories, allowing these older men to brag about their heroics and worldly conquests to some of us who had never been exposed to the wonders of the world outside our domain. One memorable evening when two of us boys were visiting the camp, one timber worker was letting his egotistic conquests get away from him, apparently to build up his self-esteem by portraying his worldly experiences for our benefit, and removing a little round rubber-like device from his pocket, joyfully boasting that he had in mind to visit the home of the farmer down the road, whose household was inhabited with a couple attractive teenage girls.

The children in our family were never told about the physical attractions that older people enjoyed, especially some of the actions that they practiced together, although we lived in a large family where this practice must have been prolific. Regardless, we were forbidden to talk about those things although we were reaching an age of curiosity about the natural inclinations of our environment. We had observed the old roosters demonstrate amorous affections in the presence of the hens from time to time, and occasionally other small animals would act friendly toward each other—but we weren't permitted to enjoy that part of nature because that stuff was evil. When we were caught observing the old rooster's amorous conduct toward a willing suitor...another dose of castor oil!

Naturally, we were curious as to the use of this little rolled-up piece of elastic, and had no idea why the farmer's daughters might be impressed with it when he visited them. When we were invited to investigate it more thoroughly, he became somewhat irritated as our curiosity was being satisfied by unrolling this unfamiliar device and trying to determine how far it would stretch! After that encounter, we walked quietly around their camp until everything was forgotten.

During the war years, while studies continued as usual, schoolchildren across the nation were engaged in collecting materials that could be used to produce arms and equipment for the armed forces. Iron materials were scarce, and many people started a vocation by building a scrap iron business. Barns, corn cribs, and other outbuildings were searched for unused metal materials, and farmers and homeowners alike sold their scrap iron to supported the war effort. Schoolchildren gathered milk seed pods to be used in making parachutes and brought them to school for further distribution.

The government needed funds to wage a global war. Ten-cent victory stamps were sold in schools, local grocery stores, post offices, and other public arenas, and all citizens were encouraged to buy as many stamps and bonds as they could afford. Celebrities performed at concerts and toured the country encouraging citizens to purchase as many war bonds and victory stamps as possible. Magazines and newspapers allotted a large amount of space in their publications to promote the sale of stamps and bonds. A short film clip persuading our citizens to buy war bonds was shown before and after feature films in the nation's theaters.

All citizens were encouraged to conserve resources, and one method of conservation enforced by the government was the rationing of scarce items. Gasoline was rationed, and persons who owned an automobile were restricted to just a few gallons each week. Tires were rationed also, and it was of utmost importance for the operator of an automobile to know how to repair flat tires, as most tires of the war period were run until they couldn't be used any further. Rarely did one take very many trips without encountering the experience of repairing a flat tire. It wasn't a big deal to have a blowout as it seldom posed a great danger when one occurred. The national speed limit of thirty-five miles per hour was enforced to save these most important resources, and when blowouts did occur, they seldom caused a serious accident. Farmers, truckers, and others who made important contributions in the manufacturing and distribution of war materials did receive an ample supply of ration stamps to operate their enterprises.

Rationing was imposed on a variety of other products, such as meats, sugar, and coffee. The coupon stamps that were allotted for these precious items were almost as important as the amount of money it took to buy the products themselves! It was common to sell gasoline, sugar, and coffee coupons for a premium, even though commerce of this kind was strictly forbidden by federal law.

As we had little means of communication, war news was passed throughout the community by word of mouth. After the broadcasting companies updated their studios to improve reception, more families began to purchase radios for their homes, and it became possible to kept up with the war news on a daily schedule, though the news was several days old. Military theme songs were played to boost the spirit of America and to honor the efforts of our soldiers. Other songs that were frequently played included those having themes with dreams depicting picturesque scenes of their loved ones coming home, or a portrait of a lover that was left behind. Some offered a portrayal of sad and unreturned love. A medley of songs that had themes of love and patriotism were quite popular during the war years and reminded us how the war had changed all phases of culture and family life.

War correspondents depicted the progress of the war each day, and some became quite famous with their battlefield reports. At the onset of the war, Hollywood began to make war films to inform the public of the heroics our soldiers were performing against the enemy. When going to the movies, a newsflash bringing the war to date would be an introduction to the feature film, and those who attended the movies regularly were kept abreast of the highlights of the news on the war front. One famous comic strip character joined the army in 1940 and became a real source of information concerning new technologies that were used in the war. Another one depicted the everyday life of the working soldiers and how they lived and contributed to the war effort.

Most communities like ours experienced an acute absence of young people, as the draft age for military service was generally between the years of eighteen and thirty-five, and most of them were soon to leave home. After loved ones had been separated for long periods of time they were afflicted with the natural urge to "go on living," as neither love, war, nor patriotism could quench the desires of those who were longing for companionship. While the young men were on the war front, it was somewhat common for sixteen- and seventeen-year-old boys to become "escorts" to older ladies for an evening's entertainment. A lad walking along a country road was eligible to receive an invitation to come in out of the cold when he traveled by the home of a lonely female who desired the affection of a male companion. Dear John letters flooded the mail as the ones back home would likely have found a local lover. Many engagements and marriages didn't make it to the end of the war.

Many of us at home were exposed to scary war stories and feared the enemy might invade our homeland, and some were so disturbed and distressed that they began having nightmares, but it all came to an end in 1945 without this fear being realized. When Germany surrendered, the children and teachers in our school assembled together on the playground to celebrate the Allied victory in Europe. This day was victorious for all, but bittersweet for those of us who had lost loved ones who would not return home after the war. The Pacific war would not end for another three months.

Our soldiers returned home within a few months

following the war, picked up their lives and helped America to return to normalcy, but many would be mentally and emotionally saddled for life with the horrors they experienced. Soldiers who were involved in combat rarely elaborated on the life they encountered on the battlefield. One neighbor boy was so disturbed by his experiences in the European theater that he had difficulty functioning as a responsible citizen, displaying the deportment of a young teenager instead of a seasoned army veteran. Others who had suffered wounds and were disabled for life began a period of rehabilitation and melted into society with constructive vocations and became responsible leaders in the community. As to those who didn't return, thousands of their names are now carved on war memorials in our towns and cities as a reminder of the sacrifices the nation suffered during those dark and uncertain days in the early forties.

Following the war, many returning servicemen and women enrolled, under the G. I. Bill, in various learning institutions to prepare themselves for a lifetime vocation. A close cousin was separated from the service in the upper forties and began training as a pilot at the local airport in Portsmouth. After he had won his license for solo flying, he was permitted to take a passenger with him. The day was beautiful, and we flew north along the Scioto River bottom land where we had, not too long ago, labored in the corn and hayfields. To the left were the three familiar peaks that guarded the eastern boundary of our homestead. We abruptly turned west when we passed the last peak. In less than a minute we were flying over our homestead at nearly one thousand feet in the air. As we traveled at ninety miles per hour, the little cleared plot of land below that had been our family's home for nearly a century seemed very small from that vantage point.

Turning left, we were soon cruising over the Scioto River and heading south. After we had climbed to nearly five thousand feet, the thrill of it all was quickly accelerated when the nose of the plane tipped over and we were looking straight down at the revolving earth. The little plane was now in a spiraling free fall, and the earth was becoming uncomfortably close. It was beginning to feel as if this passenger was sitting on a small aqueduct that ran its course down his leg to the floor of the plane. This accelerated spin continued for several minutes—well, maybe thirty seconds—before the earth below finally leveled out, leaving our hearts in a feverish thumping mode.

After flying over the Scioto River valley for a few more minutes, we glided to a halt at the end of the runway, and when all sensory systems had returned to normal it was discovered that the only aquatic system in the proximity was the Ohio River that meandered alongside the runway where the pilot was completing his flight report.

Innocence, uncertainly, inexperience, and shyness have unique ways of protecting us during the days of our youth. Even after the war had ended, men more than eighteen years of age were obligated to serve up to two years in the military services. This continuing exodus of young men left a void in the social lives of young ladies whose desires were to establish a romantic or permanent relationship with a prospective suitor. This social upheaval offered many opportunities for older teenage boys to fill the vacancy of the young men who had gone to the services, though most of us were emotionally unprepared for the role in which we found ourselves being cast.

The sawmill operator that hired a couple of us lads for summer work often invited us to accompany his family outing on Saturday nights. We frequently watched a movie in Portsmouth, and occasionally spent the evening at the pub located on the western banks of the Scioto River near Lucasville. We boys were not of age and weren't permitted to indulge in alcoholic beverages at a public establishment, but we did have a good time learning the ways of the adults and drinking soda pop, and these outings offered relief from a long week at the mill.

Later in the summer, the family decided to build a house on a wooded lot—a small acreage that was overgrown with brush and a few trees—that lay across the creek from their home. One becomes lucky to be assigned to a chore that was detestable and laborious when we had to clear new land on the hill…and the morning wasn't the most memorable to say the least, but there was to be a pleasant change ahead. While enjoying a lunch hour break in the cool shade of a couple large poplar trees near the back part of the clearing, the presence was favored by the appearance of their attractive teenage daughter fetching a glass of cool lemonade to quench the lad's midday thirst while providing a welcomed change from the morning's grubbing!

Following a few pleasantries and some small talk, the conversation got around to her morning activities. She told how she had been helping her mother prepare blackberries for canning, a perception that was quite noticeable as a large berry stain was prominent on the top of the blouse that covered of one of the well-endowed frontal projection of her upper anatomy. The conversation eventually centered on the problem of removing that big stain, after she began to lament that this was her favorite blouse and she desired to wear it when we went to the movies on Saturday night. It didn't take much of this kind of talk to cause a young boy's blood pressure to rise, and any suggestion or opinion that could be helpful took a back seat to the amorous thoughts and desires at hand.

It was true that the attendant of the grubbing patch had the inclination and the wherewithal to assist in removing the stain, but the urge to throw caution to the wind was abetted by the youthful attributes of inexperience in handling such an engagement, and the fear of lasting consequences—the last was mostly an afterthought—became a good defense if it became necessary to explain to the other boys a reason for being reluctant to participate in such an unusual proposition. However, this encounter did become a justification for bragging rights, embellished by overtones of conquest, even though it was hard to convince the other lads that this memorable noon hour really did happen. Nevertheless, the warm association that was stimulated by this encounter was a carry over to the remaining Saturday evening outings, which turned out to be very warm ones indeed.

15. Our Neighborhood

The general population of Morgan Township was an assortment of emigrants from the eastern and southern states, and the people were predisposed to conservative ideas in religion and public affairs, mostly stemming from the customs and mores handed down by their parents and, most important, the economic conditions of the times. Being from a backwoods rural area, education was not a big priority in their lives, and young people were deemed successful if they married, raised a family, and established a vocation in farming or in the operation of a small business. A small segment of the population worked in factories and in the retail industry in Portsmouth. Newly married couples got their start in life by living with their parents for a spell, although this sometimes caused difficulty in the family.

Many communities settled along larger creeks that meandered through the rolling hills, with primitive roads crossing the creeks to give access to their homes with horse and wagon and, in later years, automobiles. These roads crossed creek beds without the benefit of culverts or bridges, and became impassable for a few days when hard rains caused flash floods that inundated the creek beds and low areas nearby. To have permanent access to their homes they built swinging bridges—just wide enough for a person to walk—across the creeks where they intersected with paths that afforded access to their homes.

People rarely built their homes over basements as it was much easier to construct a nearby building for storage area. Wood was the common fuel for heating and cooking, but some eventually turned to coal when economic conditions permitted. The furniture was most common, consisting of crude straight-backed and rocking chairs, as overstuffed furniture was really a luxury. The style of the furniture wasn't all that important because people worked outdoors a large portion of the day, excepting in cold and inclement weather, as working days were truly from dawn to dusk.

Seldom did we see a new home being built in the community, but when older structures such as a one-room schoolhouse or a township building were vacated, it wasn't long before a family made arrangements to acquire that structure and turn it into their new home. Fenced-in yards were the playgrounds for children and the ground would likely be bare where they played outdoor games. In some instances, homeowners might stake out a calf or goat in the yard to control the grass in other areas. Eventually a few lawn mowers appeared, but they were laborious to use, as the only mowers at that time were the small reel type pushed by hand. Only a few families in the neighborhood used these mowers, as there were more urgent problems to be solved than mowing grass.

Without any expertise in family planning, most families of that day were generally quite large. It was common for a couple to have six to eight children or more born into the family. The local schools and churches, the main social institutions in the area, were enhanced with enrollment as each family grew toward the stages of maturity, and four or five children from the same family might be enrolled in the institutions at the same time. This could be good or bad for the younger siblings of the family, as the conduct and deportment of older members would have an influence on the younger ones. Social clubs, such as the Farm Bureau, Grange, health clubs, or even card clubs, were seldom organized to entertain or promote the welfare of the community. Society as a whole was mostly centered within the individual families, having little intercourse in formal social structures that would have enhanced the well-being of both families and community.

Our closest neighbor lived just across the ridge to the north of our home place, but we seldom visited or worked with them, and Dad was somewhat silent concerning his relationship with that family. His sister married into the family in the early twentieth century and died about twelve years later, without having children. We often wondered if this marriage caused differences that may have kept our associations on the cool side, and though relations did thaw somewhat between us children during the early forties, it cannot be recalled that the adults warmed up to each other that much. Cordial pleasantries were offered when a member of their clan passed by our home on the way to Bear Creek.

A grumpy old man lived on the bank just a few yards from the store. We boys referred to him as "snake." He was a tall, lanky gentleman who believed that life hadn't treated him very well, as he seemed to come up short most of the time in dealing with others. Sometimes his contentious disposition would get him into trouble with his neighbors, as he often accused them of committing petty acts against him, and especially would retaliate against young boys who might find pleasure in trying to agitate him. We mostly steered clear of his way, but one Christmas holiday when school had been dismissed for vacation, a confrontation surfaced between the gentleman and some of the local teens, probably instigated by the younger ones. In his desire to bring about justice for this run-in, he filed charges in the juvenile courts against the lads for disturbing the peace and the destruction of his property.

When the deputy sheriff began to investigate the complaint, it was discovered that one of the boys had been in Cincinnati for the holidays and was wrongly accused. This finding caused the deputy to question the accuser if he really knew any of the boys who had been in the mischief, or if he just picked several names of those he knew loafed around together. It was quickly determined that the latter was the case, and all charges were dropped. After being declared innocent on a technicality, we walked quietly by his home following that encounter and gave him more room as we didn't desire to get into any more trouble with the law.

A neighbor who lived alongside the area where our road connected to the highway was a farmer, trader, and trucker, among other things. He owned one of the early steel-wheeled tractors and did most of his farming with it. Seldom did he farm with horses, supposedly because they required a lot of care and farming was more difficult when the work was done with horses than it was with the tractor.

The road from the highway leading to our house began in the corner of the neighbor's property. It intersected the highway in a low area near the river and immediately crossed a small creek before it began an accent toward the hill. When floods occurred on the Scioto River, this section of our road would become inundated with back water, cutting off passage to the highway, and we had to walk through a neighbor's field to reach the highway. It would have been more convenient had the road been routed along a hillside and away from the lowland, but nothing ever came to fruition.

A large portion of our road meandered alongside this neighbor's property, and had been in the same location for nearly seventy-five years, well before the present owner came on the scene. However, it appeared that he seized every opportunity to inform us children that the road was really his because it was routed over his property. Whether he desired to provoke dissension or was just playing tricks with us kids, he would occasionally broach the subject concerning the ownership of the road. One time, believing we might be desirous that the road be relocated, he suggested to one of us boys that Dad should sue him for a new right-of-way! We believed he was purposely bringing this idea to surface in order to incite doubt about the legality of our road, but it didn't work in his favor as we had no reason to pursue something we already possessed. The right-of-way was a bone of contention between us but the subject never developed into open confrontation. Our oldest brother married into the family in the late thirties, which may have eased tensions to some degree.

Citizens in the community who were fortunate enough to own automobiles were generally employed in city factories or held jobs having a steady income, and would accommodate others in need by providing transportation during emergencies. Those who owned an automobile might be persuaded to make a run to the grocery store, providing their own cupboards were in need of restocking—and for a small fee. A few small farmers and day laborers who owned automobiles traveled to the larger stores in town, but others without means to patronize the larger stores, like us, were obliged to shop at the small country stores where staples were a little more costly.

The farmers along the river bottoms began to acquire tractors equipped with steel wheels and used them for the purpose of plowing ground and doing other heavy work, but a team of horses or a span of mules was the mainstay on planting and cultivation.

These steel wheels on the tractors, having numerous and sharp lugs for traction, were very destructive on roadways, especially on the macadam roads that had only a thin surface of asphalt. One or two passages on such roads could cause the surface to crumble and create numerous potholes. Eventually rubber tires became standard equipment on tractors, allowing them to travel on the roads, which increased their utility in most phases of farming. Cultivators were eventually installed on tractors, and later, when the primitive one-row corn pickers emerged, they were effective in turning the working animals out to pasture. The downside of this technology was the increase in the rate of unemployment among farm workers.

The tractor was scarcely seen among the hill farmers until the forties, and upland farmers continued to rely on horses for farm work. The riding plow, pulled by three or four horses, was a great improvement in preparing the soil for planting, and riding cultivators relieved the farmer from considerable walking during the hot weather when cultivating corn. A farm family could eke out a living on a few acres by growing enough feed for the work horses, three or four milk cows, and a hundred laying hens, as a good portion of the family income was generated by selling milk, cream, butter, and eggs.

The Ohio Canal that lay along the Scioto River had been abandoned since the turn of the century, and a few of the more well-to-do residents of Portsmouth acquired a small acreage of land located between the canal and the river. They built small cottages overlooking the river and would occasionally weekend in the country, fishing, relaxing, or improving their property. A few kept their surroundings quite attractive by painting their cottages, building fences, planting small gardens, and growing flowers. While we didn't travel in their social circles, a few of them were quite friendly toward us as we ventured by their cottages.

Late winter or early spring rains resulted in major flooding, as the Corps of Engineers had not yet built flood control dams along the Scioto River, the main artery that drained water from thousands of square miles of land in the northern part of the state. When the river did go on a rampage, especially if heavy rain came in the winter when the ground was frozen, all low-lying roads were closed and those cottages were inundated with the flood water, as it often rose to or near the roofs of some of them. After the flood subsided, the cottage owners encountered a major clean-up, as flood water deposited large quantities of mud in their weekend retreats. Yet very few cottages would become vacant and those river floods were just another obstacle to overcome so that the pleasures of quiet country weekends might be enjoyed!

Most roads were laid alongside creeks and were

periodically improved with gravel to build a solid road base. During the winter months when freezing and thawing occurred, wagon wheels cut deep ruts in the road and it required constant work to keep them passable. With the event of the automobile, extra gravel was needed to produce a better road base, but with constant use, the road bed became rutty like a washboard and would make a rough ride in those old cars. The roads were dragged quite often in an attempt to keep them passable, but this wasn't very successful. Eventually, road graders became standard pieces of equipment for the township governments.

During dry periods, these roads seemingly turned to dust, and families living near a gravel road were constantly cleaning their homes, especially if these homes were structured downwind from the road, as a moderately speeding automobile would leave a trail of dust that seemingly had no other place to go accept into their houses through open windows! Later on, the highway department acquired tanker trucks and spread an oil-based solution on the road near people's homes to control the dust. The main highways were becoming macadamized, but the quality of the product, the base of the road bed, and the thin layer that was applied seldom offered permanent improvements. Come spring, after freezing and thawing, the road would become full of pot holes and in need of major repair.

Public utilities were seldom available in rural areas, but eventually these services were extended to outlying areas, and rural people began to enjoy the amenities that had only been available in the cities. Electricity was one of the first major utilities to appear, but our community was one of the last to experience strung wire hanging from tall poles. The houses that were connected to the power lines were wired by snaking lines through the space between the outer and inner walls to feed a light receptacle, generally positioned in the center of the ceiling. Very few plug-in receptacles were installed as there weren't many electrical appliances on the market. Early on, most people were happy with having just a few electric lights, but as more household appliances became available, house wiring techniques improved to accommodate the need.

Telephone wires were strung less than a mile from our lane, but in general the telephone didn't become a household item until well in the decade of the forties. Persons desiring to contact family members living in a distant town would be obliged to travel to the nearest village to make a call, although this was seldom done except in emergencies, and often the person one desired to contact most likely didn't have a home phone. It was a custom to give out a neighbor's number so that contact could be made in emergencies.

One local entrepreneur attempted to start a movie house in his filling station. Having acquired a motion picture camera, he somehow obtained an old film, and for just a few cents we could enjoy the movies on Saturday evenings during the summer. This enterprise didn't get off the ground, but it was a beginning that helped to open the door to more diverse cultural activities.

Ever so slowly, the people living in the northern sections of our county began to emerge from a culture resembling pioneer living to that of modern times. Following the war years, it became a profitable venture for the various utilities to extend their services into rural areas where the niceties of city life were enjoyed by those living in the country.

Near the end of the forties, our family, whose numbers had dwindled to just four persons, wasn't a beneficiary of the necessities that many of our neighbors were beginning to enjoy. We were stuck in a rut, primarily as our home was located a mile or more from any utility, making it impossible for us to enjoy the amenities that others began to refer to as necessities. The face of the nation was changing, but our way of life would not have been indistinguishable from that of our ancestors who settled the land nearly one hundred years earlier.

16. A Family Left Behind

The period of the twenties, thirties and early forties, despite the Depression and high unemployment, did advance with technological improvements, but many farm laborers and unskilled workers suffered, as these changes were responsible for temporary unemployment. The automobile and truck were becoming dependent means of transportation, but their utility challenged the livelihood of thousands of day laborers. The tractor soon replaced the work horses, and the combine laid the threshing gangs by the wayside. The old one-row corn picker could pick more corn in a day than ten men could husk by hand. Laborers who earned their living working on farms became infuriated with these inventions and wanted to retaliate against the progressive changes that threatened their way of life. Farmers were scorned by some who had become unemployed because of the introduction of modern machinery, and many had to guard their barns and equipment to protect them from being burned.

The great war brought unparalleled changes to the lives of all Americans. Young men and women were conscripted into the armed forces and were faced with the reality of separation from their families. Employment became available for most able-bodied people and they were encouraged to relocate in the nation's manufacturing centers where war materials were being produced. Those employed to produce vital materials for the war were generally frozen on that job and had to remain there for the duration. Millions of women who previously had little political persuasion and had never worked outside the home entered the manufacturing sector and were quite instrumental in changing the structure of our social, political, and industrial activities.

In retrospect, some may have thought our family should have moved from the hill and found greener pastures to enhance our status of living, but we owned a land that had the necessary natural resources for survival and it was possible to eke out a living, however meager. Change would have been almost impossible, as we didn't have the resources to start a new life elsewhere.

Ours was a family that had deep roots in a land that had been called home for the most part of a century. Dad was well into the middle to upper age limits of life, and with several young members of the family still at home, and having the responsibility of providing for Grandma's welfare, he was simply trapped by the circumstances of that time. For him there appeared to be little choice but to remain on the hill until each of us children grew into a state of responsibility and began to exit the homeland, one by one. Fittingly, it was Father, living alone—and tired—approaching the age of seventy years, who was the last to leave the hill farm in early 1951, bringing to close the last chapter of those memorable years—when we were growing up.

We children have been asked many times if there were any lasting effects on members of the clan who lived the aforementioned way of life. In a sense, our response might be compared to the millions of armed service people in World War II who quietly came home, went to work, and began to put their lives back in order. Our family was of the same generation, and our dreams didn't encounter any other option.

Random conversation has revealed that deep feelings still exist to some degree concerning our childhood years. Early on, our parents were strict, using backwoods disciplinary measures, sometimes physical, to keep the pack in line. They required compulsory church attendance—without regard to personal desires—in adherence with the mores of society and the beliefs of their forefathers. Whether this mode of life changed the idealism of family members or not, this fact will never be determined. Ironically, most older siblings more or less shunned the importance of the church while most of the younger members have adhered to its teachings. One might conclude that the importance of the church is a toss-up in personal values of the individual members of the family.

With our economic background and educational opportunities, it might be assumed that we would have blended into the surroundings where we grew up and lived a rural life occasional to that area, but this was not to be. The independence we acquired in that backwoods setting became an asset when we left the security of the land, and each of us eventually assumed responsibility in our chosen profession and in society in general, all foreign to our previous way of life.

We were certainly influenced with a conviction of a strong family lifestyle. Of the five remaining siblings who have lived well into the eighth and ninth decades of life, one has celebrated more than sixty years of matrimony, while three of us can boast of more than fifty years—with the same spouses—and if not for an untimely accident, one more would have most assuredly achieved this accomplishment. Disease and death were the causes of the untimely separations of two marriages in the family, and one...well, every family, especially a large one, sports a member who could be referred to as a free spirit. He was definitely the most carefree one of the clan, and maybe the happiest.

Each of us could be identified as strong-willed, fiercely competitive, and strongly opinionated, along with a little temper in the mix. When compared to our progenitors, one doesn't have to be too well-schooled in the history of genetic influence to realize we were chips off the block, some favoring the temperamental attributes of Mom's family, others demonstrating the milder manner of Dad's family. Time reveals all things, but in spite of—or because of—the circumstances we encountered, one might determine that Dad and Mom did as well, maybe better, in bringing up a socially adjusted family as did their offspring.

The Players

Robert McElhaney, our grandfather, born Feb. 7, 1857, in Wetzel Co., Virginia (today's West Virginia), lived in the Sedan area until he brought his young family to the hill farm in the early 1890s, probably a move to help care for his brothers and sisters who were struggling to survive on the farm. It appears that he wasn't much more successful on the farm than his parents, who first homesteaded the hill following the Civil War. Robert lived thirty-five years on the farm, toiling the land and raising his family, and died in 1929 at the age of 72 years.

Surilda Walls McElhaney, our grandmother, was born March 4, 1861, on Camp Creek, and lived her youth on upper Sedan before marrying Robert. This union resulted in five adult children, three of which matured to raise their own families, with Father being one of them. Following the death of Robert, she continued to live in the original home until she became an invalid and lived with her daughter until her death in 1948.

George McElhaney, our father, born on upper Bear Creek on Sept. 29, 1884, whose life has been depicted throughout the pages of our story, lived on the homestead all but a few years of his life. Following the youngest child's departure from the hill farm, Father married Janie Jones, with whom he lived on Bear Creek until her death in 1955. In 1957, he married Ada Seaman of Peebles, Ohio, and lived with her until his death in 1966. He is buried in the family plot in the Howard Cemetery on Camp Creek, Pike County, just a couple of miles from our original home place.

Myrtle Ealey McElhaney, our mother, born in Johnson County, Kentucky, Dec. 9, 1897, left Kentucky when her family moved to Bear Creek. In 1916, she married George McElhaney. Together they built their home on the hill and she was to become the mother of fifteen children, with only nine living to maturity. Our mother died with childbirth in July 1938, having lived with Father only twenty-two years. She is buried in the family plot at the Howard Cemetery.

George Franklin McElhaney, born November 24, 1916, was married to Grace Picklesimer of Lucasville in 1938. They were childless. Frank worked in the community until he was drafted into the Army in 1943, and was subsequently assigned to the Army Air Force and stationed at a training facility somewhere in England, with a mission to ferry troops behind the enemy lines in France. In June 1944, during the invasion of Normandy, his squadron had made several successful missions into France, but on June 25, 1944, the aircraft of which he was a crew member crashed in an attempt to deliver supplies to the front and retrieve a glider plane. He is interred in Cambridge Cemetery, Cambridge, England.

Mary McElhaney, born January 31, 1918, lived all of her life with the family, excepting a period when she was occasionally employed in domestic work during her teenage years. Mary was afflicted with diabetes early on, a disease that was to take her life just two days short of nineteen years. She died on January 29, 1937, and is buried in the family plot at Howard Cemetery.

Leonard (Ray) McElhaney was born May 29, 1920, and married Dorothy Green of Lucasville in September 1939. Following the outbreak of World War II—being ineligible for the armed services, as he was afflicted with diabetes—Ray moved his family to Rittman, Ohio, and worked at the Ohio Box Board, becoming an administrator in the distribution department. He died at Dad's home in Peebles, Ohio, on September 6, 1960, and is buried in the Burbank Cemetery, Burbank, Ohio.

Burl McElhaney, born October 16, 1923, served in the U.S. Army during World War II. He married Margaret Swearingen in 1943, and after being discharged from the military service, began a career in watch repairing. He later trained in the field of electronics and worked many years at the Florida Space Center, being shop superintendent of a department that supported the Bomarc, Minuteman, Saturn 5 Apollo, Russian Soyus Hookup, and the space shuttle programs. He is now retired and lives in Florida.

Leon McElhaney, born July 2, 1927, was drafted by the army and became a military police officer. Following his discharge, he married Ollie Riley in 1947, and worked at the Ohio Box Board at Rittman, Ohio. Soon thereafter, he entered the ministry and has been active in that endeavor for nearly fifty years. Leon moved his family to Lake City, Florida, and during the early seventies started a business in sales and repair for small household appliances. He is retired and lives in Lake City, Florida.

Robert McElhaney, born July 22, 1929, married Nora Burger in 1950, and chose automobile technology as his vocation. He worked in Columbus, Ohio, several years before moving his family to Orlando, Florida, during the middle fifties, where he continued working in his chosen profession until he died in 1987.

David McElhaney, born March 30, 1931, after graduating from high school, enlisted into the U.S. Navy in early 1951, and was engaged in the Korean theater for nearly four years. He married Charlotte Shelton in 1952. Following his discharge, he attended and graduated from Wilmington College and began a career in coaching, teaching, and administration in the public schools in Ohio. He retired from the River View School District in 1984 and now lives at Coshocton, Ohio.

Artie McElhaney, born June 27, 1932, after graduating from High School, married Charles Boldman and raised her family near McDermott, Ohio. She later became employed by the local school district as manager of the cafeterias in the district. Artie, the only member of the family who chose to live in the vicinity where we grew up, is retired and lives in the McDermott, Ohio, area.

Paul McElhaney, born May 1, 1934, married Nellie Stanley in 1955. He served in the U.S. Army in the European theater during the late fifties. In 1980, Nellie was involved in a fatal automobile accident. Paul worked in Columbus, Ohio, as a milling machine operator until his retirement. He is at present a pastor of a church in Columbus and is married to Janis McElhaney. They live at Johnston, Ohio.

FIFTY YEARS LATER....

After leaving the hill as a lad of eighteen years, I didn't return to the farm again, excepting a few times to visit my father before entering the U.S. Navy in January 1951. Although I had been in the vicinity many times, I had little desire to revisit the scene of those formidable years. It was nearly fifty years later that I returned, accompanied by my wife Charlotte and our three living children, Kenneth, Duane, and Evelyn. My sister Artie, who lives in the area, and her family made the trek with us. The original road that led to the hill from the Scioto Valley had long ago been abandoned, and we walked to the hill from the Bear Creek side of the farm on a newly bulldozed road that afforded passage, constructed by the state of Ohio, the present owner.

As we entered the vicinity of the homestead, everything was quite unfamiliar, although I had spent a long eighteen years there. The newly cut road ended almost at the exact spot where our home once stood, and the only identifying landmark at that site was the large white oak tree that had previously guarded our house near the corner of the patio.

Most other identifying landmarks had long been destroyed or obscured with heavy foliage. All buildings, including our two houses, had long ago been razed. The old road at the edge of our yard was overgrown with underbrush, and the garden and potato patches were now graced with pine trees standing nearly fifty feet tall. The fruit trees and grape arbors, which had provided such an important supplement to our diet, were no longer in competition for space with the large oak tree that sheltered a favorite playground area and anchored the western corner of our yard.

As we ambled toward the sight where Grandma lived, we walked over an identifying mound and noted that it wasn't nearly as tall or steep as it appeared to have been when as youngsters we coasted our homemade wagon over its side, dragging our feet on the ground in an attempt to stop before we ran into the creek.

The area where Grandma's house once stood, and where so many family memories were born, is now just a small plot of ground that is overgrown with briars and saplings. The well, near the corner of the house, was surrounded with briars and scrub brush; its opening was covered with a pile of brush that afforded little if any protection to a hunter or other persons unfamiliar with its location. A small pit in the ground, once walled with large basement stones, identified the area of the cellar where our families had stored their winter provisions of fruit, vegetables, and potatoes for nearly a hundred years. The majestic oak tree that once graced the western side of her house had long ago fallen, with only the deteriorating shell of the prostrate trunk giving witness to its previous existence. We were unable to find any trace of the fence that once established the parameter of our yards and enclosed our pasture fields.

As I gazed toward the area where the chimney once

adorned the end of Grandma's house, I was reminded that the swallows no longer had a refuge in which to build their nests. In the nearby woods, the whippoorwill has for many years been snuggling into its nest each evening without anyone hearing her last song of the day.

When I viewed the surroundings from that vantage point, it was easily to observe that the wells that had been dug near small creeks were silted nearly full with soil that had eroded from upstream creek beds. The cornfields had grown into a wilderness of oak, maple and pine trees, and the pasture fields were now a forest, with the trees crowding out the berry patches from which we plucked our winters' fruit.

The only road that bisected the property was showing signs of advanced deterioration with briars, small trees, and erosion all assisting in its demise. Fallen trees blocked the road at many places, causing our passage to be more difficult as we attempted to explore the more memorable sites of yesteryear.

Following the path that led to the top of the hill to the west of our house, I became aware of the silence displayed by our children, seemingly taking in the aura of yesteryear in wonder, no doubt contemplating the differences of the cultures of just one generation. I was pleased to become reacquainted with the many beech, hickory, oak, and poplar trees that provided a home for the squirrels. A squawk of a red squirrel hanging on the side of a large beech tree, whether a homecoming welcome or a warning of danger to its friends, brought back fond memories of the many hours that I had sat among those sprawling giants with Dad's old single-barrel shotgun in my arms waiting in an attempt to take home an evening meal.

As we prepared to make the trek back to the highway, we paused alongside the giant white oak tree that was still standing on the bank just a few yards to the west of

Grandma's house. Three generations of McElhaney children had played under the boughs of that great tree, climbed its trunk and sat on its branches. We tied our swings to the large limbs that protruded horizontally from its trunk, played tin-can hockey in its shade, and coasted our homemade wagon down the slope at its side. That old stately tree had met its match with nature, and lost. It is possible that the years of loneliness and old age played a part in its demise. In a few more years, its roots will lose the strength to hold it upright, and in the near future, visitors will observe how Father Time commands its own order in the restoration of the earth that man....

Slowly but surely, the forces of nature are returning the homestead to its pristine state. All that remains are the memories of the families of four generations that toiled for nearly a century to survive and propagate new generations.

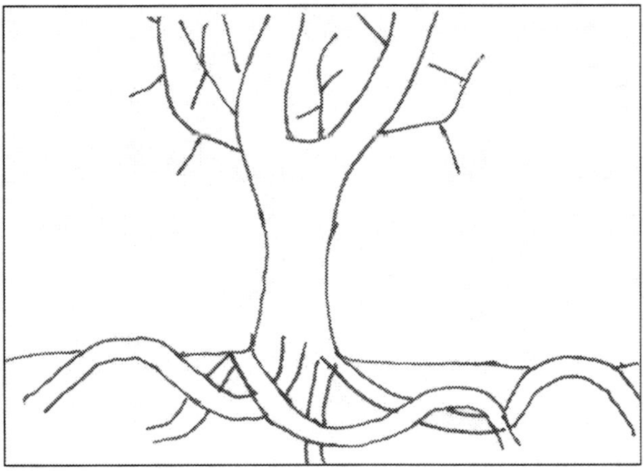

Printed in the United States
91518LV00004B/138/A